Paper Bride

Nava Semel (b. 1954, Tel Aviv, Israel) holds an MA in Art History and is an art critic. Semel has worked as a TV, radio and recording producer and as a journalist. She has written poetry, prose for children and adults, television scripts and opera libretti, in addition to translating plays. Semel has received several literary prizes, including the American National Jewish Book Award for children's literature (1990), the Women Writers of the Mediterranean Award (1994), the Austrian Best Radio Drama Award (1996), the Israeli Prime Minister's Award (1996) and Tel Aviv Woman of the Year in Literature Award (2007). Her latest novel in Hebrew is *Screwed on Backwards* (2011).

Also by Nava Semel (in translation)

Becoming Gershona
Flying Lessons
Bride on Paper
Hat of Glass
Love for Beginners
Who Stole the Show?
The Child Behind the Eyes
And the Rat Laughed

Paper Bride

Nava Semel

Translated from Hebrew
by
Sondra Silverston

HYBRID
PUBLISHERS

Published by Hybrid Publishers

Melbourne Victoria Australia

©2012

Hybrid Publishers
PO Box 52, Ormond 3204.
www.hybridpublishers.com.au

English-language edition first published 2012

National Library of Australia
Cataloguing-in-Publication data:
Author: Semel, Nava
Title: Paper Bride/Nava Semel

ISBN: 9781921665561 (pbk)

Dewey Number: 892.437
Typeset in Baskerville 11.5/14.6

Uzik

I won't live forever. That thought, which seemed so obvious, struck me sharply when I tried to make a movie for the first time.

I tried to correct the flawed, cruel landscape reflected in the lens. A ridiculous attempt to compensate for small injustices, but even so, I couldn't give it up.

I am not the main character of this story. All my life, I have always preferred to look at things through the transparent shield of a camera, using it as an intermediary to protect myself. I don't pretend to include everything. The narrow strip of celluloid time has indeed been fastened onto the spinning reel, but I found a way—although not an especially original one—to interrupt and alter the arbitrary flow of the screening.

I sometimes wonder if that really was my life, and I'm afraid that one day, I'll discover that the most important things were left on the cutting room floor.

In the end, I did not succeed in finding the image that would truthfully represent the grand words. I closed my eyes in despair a thousand times, as I tried to convey love of homeland in a tangible image. Words, after all, were never enough for me. Even when you arrange them this way or that, they never tell the exact story you want, and the story too, no matter how faithful it is, changes before your very eyes, as if another director were interfering in your work. Is what I described what actually happened?

I, like everyone else, have the right to be skeptical.

How arrogant it is to move through time as if it were my own personal possession. To appropriate my own story, to tear off pieces of other people's memories, interspersing them with the opaque strips of film we call "leaders." Methods have improved. Something new comes onto the scene every day, and confusion grows. I don't fool myself that I'll ever be able to bridge the gaps between the black strip and the white screen. If I made a bad bargain in my choices, this is my last chance to correct them, because what I choose to tell is what will remain, Zionka. And you asked me to learn one more lesson that had nothing to do with letters and words. The day will come—if it does—when I learn to forgive myself.

One year in the life of a dog is equivalent to seven years of human life. That too is a strip of time spinning out on another reel. I've had endless conversations on the subject, but I still haven't discovered whether dogs also find it difficult to reconcile themselves to the terrifying fact that they can't live forever. I don't know if any of the dogs I had, any of my Johnny Weissmullers, ever weighed the balance of good and bad in their lives, or regretted what they had missed.

There are many ways to tell this story, and mine is not necessarily the right one. When the reel spins on the projector, and the last picture flickers in the air, practically slipping back into the projectionist's hands, I ask myself if what I have done was worth doing. I ask, and will keep on asking again and again, whether there is a person there.

Obcinać in Polish, *ikta* in Arabic. As for the Hebrew word, we never use it. How strange we use only the English "CUT".

Chapter 1

Whenever someone asked me what my family does for the homeland—a question people never stopped asking in Palestine—I always answered immediately—"We get married." I remember the first time I said it and my teacher threw me out of the class. He tried to get control of himself, silencing the first giggles with a threatening gesture. Banished, I stood near the principal's office, my teacher's note of complaint in my hand. Even though it was folded in a sealed envelope, I managed to take it out, careful not to tear the envelope. I tried to get someone to read the words for me, and Zionka was the only one who would do it.

"Uziel has dishonored our people and our homeland," the note said. Zionka was embarrassed. She lowered her eyes as if she were the guilty party. She could barely get the words out, and not because she had some kind of reading problem like I did.

And so, dear children, we repeat the question. What does your family do for the homeland? Herzl Fleisher stood up first, followed by other pupils, all of them describing how their fathers or their uncles or other people they knew were active in the defense of the Jews in Palestine or had devoted their lives to building the country. But I hadn't lied. My big brother Imri really did go to Poland to get married for the homeland.

His first bride was Anna.

The night Imri left, he went to the toolshed, opened the rusty metal locks of the old brown valise lying near the clay pots once used as bee hives, and emptied out his old school notebooks. Imri too had once been a kid, though that was sometimes hard for me to believe. Aunt Miriam says that he was the most outstanding student in the history of our village and made our mother and father very proud. They expected great things from him. That's what Aunt Miriam told anyone who was willing to listen. To me, she used to say, "How lucky they're not alive to see how you've turned out."

Imri filled the valise with clothes that had been lying around the shed since our father died. Watching him trying to fold our father's best, English-made black suit and two wrinkled, white silk shirts, I began to laugh.

"Imri," I asked, "are you going to a fancy dress ball?"

Then he stood in front of the small, cracked mirror he had hung on a hook and practiced knotting a tie. He kept getting a different, peculiar-looking knot every time, and I said he looked like a condemned prisoner who had volunteered to tie his own noose. But he wasn't offended at all. He simply bent down in front of the small mirror, hunting for the exact spot where his head ended and his neck began and mumbling, "It'll work. It has to work."

Imri didn't pack his real clothes. There were none of the khaki pants and sleeveless undershirts Aunt Miriam mended every Saturday night. I don't know where he found Daddy's ironed handkerchiefs. I was sure Aunt

Miriam had given them to the Sephardic old age home in Jerusalem a long time ago.

He reeked of mothballs. I wrinkled my nose and said, "Imri, be careful these clothes don't change you," and he replied dismissively, "Clothes are just pieces of material loosely sewn together. What's inside never changes." When he was finally satisfied with the knot he had tied, he tightened it, stood up and said, "As for you, Uzik, take care of the house and the hives. And especially of Aunt Miriam."

I tried to look directly into his eyes, but couldn't. He was too busy locking the valise and dragging it out of the shed, giving me orders the whole time as if I were a stranger. Don't forget to feed the chickens and lock the gate to the yard with the heavy padlock every single night. Remember to pay Mohammed Daudi for his work on the first of every month, and be careful a swarm of bees doesn't attack when you open the cover of the hive and fold back the burlap sack sticky with propolis and wax. And never ever go near the English air base that borders our land. And if anybody asks where your older brother has disappeared to, tell them he's taken a boat to Italy to bring back some less aggressive, stingless queen bees that will produce thicker honey than ours do.

It was a long list, and I only half-listened. He didn't mention school, maybe because he knew it was hopeless. Finally, just before two strangers arrived in a van to pick him up, he said, "And promise me you won't cause any trouble. No pranks while I'm gone," and added as an afterthought, "It'll be worth your while. I'll bring you a present from Europe."

Wearing striped pajamas that were once Imri's, I watched them pull away. I didn't understand why he had to leave me alone with Aunt Miriam for such a long time. He was hardly ever home as it was. I was furious at the people from the Jewish Agency who had sent him on a mission right before the harvesting season. And most of all, I was afraid he was leaving me for a place where mysterious, incomprehensible things happen that have nothing at all to do with bees and honey. I ran after the van, calling, "Imri, Imri, don't go!" When he didn't answer, I shouted, "Something terrible's going to happen and it'll be your fault!" But my shouts were in vain. Either Imri didn't hear me or he chose to ignore my threats.

The van rocked its way along the narrow dirt road behind our yard. I saw the two strangers clap him on the back and heard them laugh loudly. One of them said, "There are such beauties waiting for you there," and I recalled what Zionka's mother said about elegant and educated European women. I hoped none of them would agree to have a boyfriend who smelled of mothballs. The sound of singing drifted over from the English air base, and I knew that the pilots were polishing off another one of the cases of beer they bought in Shmariyahu's grocery in our village every morning.

I sat on the floor of the toolshed. The lighted kerosene lamp scattered the old smells. Imri isn't especially neat, but Aunt Miriam never yells at him about it. Our father's old clothes were strewn all around. I couldn't remember him ever wearing such fancy clothes. I gathered them into a pile, and didn't find even one piece of women's clothing. I smelled the mothballs for a minute, making an effort to remember. But I gave it up immediately. I'd be late for school again and my teacher would say, "So, what can you expect from Uzik the troublemaker."

I could've pulled a trick or two to delay Imri. If I'd taken the air out of the van's tires, or opened a hive and let the bees out, then maybe he would have had to cancel his trip. But it was too late now.

———

What did you do for your homeland?

I'm sure the principal suspected me of opening the envelope on the sly and getting someone to read the complaint note to me. He and the teachers have insinuated more than once that I really do know how to read. They think I'm purposely putting on an act just to annoy them.

The principal sighed, "What are we going to do with you, Uziel? I hope this is the last time you carry on this way. We'll have no choice but to leave you back a grade. Some day, you'll learn that our homeland is not a joke."

I tried to guess what kind of punishment was in store for me. Anything but having to write a hundred times in my notebook, "Our homeland is not a joke." I couldn't even write that sentence once, let alone a hundred times. I'd have to ask Zionka to do it for me. She has such beautiful handwriting. She's always getting compliments on her neat, round letters. But when I look in her notebook, I can never tell what's on the page and what's run off the edges.

To my surprise, the principal simply raised his glance from the large diary that lay open in front of him and said, "Tell your brother I wish him a very successful trip."

A single tie lay on the toolshed floor. An orphaned snake, like the kind I find during the summer near the gate of the English air base. I put it around my neck and tried to make a knot like Imri's. The small mirror was still hanging on its hook. I looked into the crack and saw myself broken into pieces. I narrowed my eyes above the flickering face inside the small frame and said, "Shut up." I was sorry I hadn't hugged Imri goodbye, like in the movies. He's my only brother. I don't have any others. And it immediately occurred to me that, in the movies, only lovers hug that way when they know they'll never see each other again. Imri, who had already seen quite a few movies, hates that kind of ending. The girl always whines and waves her handkerchief, looking sniffly and miserable.

There wasn't even one handkerchief in the whole pile of Daddy's clothes. Imri had taken them all to blow his nose into or wipe his sweat with. Zionka's mother is impressed by Imri's manners. She says he's "absolutely European," and that's exactly why I prefer my sleeve.

My face in the mirror was squashed. For a minute, I looked like a whining girl. Even the tie hung pathetically from my neck because the knot was too loose. What a horrible beginning. The words kept echoing in my mind, "Our homeland is not a joke, not a joke ..." I blew out the flame of the kerosene lamp with one breath.

Back then, I still didn't know Anna.

Imri

What do I know about women? The mission I've under-
taken is more difficult than I imagined. I shouldn't have
agreed. But they pleaded with me. For the sake of the
homeland, they said. After all, what did I have to do? It's
a trivial matter to say, "Thou art consecrated unto me by
the law of Moses and Israel" and then break the glass.
Later, we get divorced and I never see her again. It's all
arranged in advance, each of us relying on the good will
of the other.

Many men endanger their lives for the sake of noble
ideas, and I'm not even risking my liberty. I only *seem* to
be doing so. Getting my passport stamped requires no
great effort on my part. And yet that faint imprint will
bind me to a woman I've never seen before, in a place
whose name I've never heard. Teach me, Aharonchik.

I'll have to be alone with her and I don't even know
if she's attractive. What will I do if she smells bad or acts
strangely? Should I open doors for her, bring her flowers,
call her by her first name, and what will I do if, God help
me, we touch each other or if I'm forced to put my arm
around her shoulders to convince the authorities that
she really is my wife?

Now, contemplating the moment we stand face to
face, nothing separating us, I'm filled with anxiety. The
two of us in the hold of a ship, the compartment narrow and stifling, its round porthole like the window of

a prison cell, the black sea rocking us. And I drink in the breath of that stranger lying in the bunk beside me. You could've stopped me, Aharonchik. I must have lost my mind. How naïve I am! I may have read many books, but I'm not familiar with that intricate game a man and a woman play. She'll bear my name, and even after I give her the divorce, the paper will bleed with her memory. No one ever taught me how to act with a woman. They teach you everything but that. How do you make love?

Chapter 2

In the village, they call me "Uzik the troublemaker" because of the things I do, which they call "pranks," and when the village rabbi wants to console Aunt Miriam, he calls them "a bit of mischief," as if a different name could change what it means. My pranks, I explain to Zionka, aren't dangerous to anyone and have never yet caused anybody to run away from Palestine.

I think everyone around me is too serious. They work from sunrise to sunset in the cow sheds, in the citrus groves and with the beehives, and they never leave their small stores, even on the hottest days. When we celebrate a special occasion in the village, like a wedding, they cry on the bride's shoulder, trot out all the troubles they've had in the past, and recall all the dead people who martyred themselves for some cause or other. Especially Aunt Miriam, who keeps her feet propped up on a footstool the whole evening, sighing, "Life is hard."

So, I look for ways to be happy. Most of all, I want to make myself laugh, and sometimes, I think that only a prank can prove I exist.

Aharonchik, the baker, who is the most ardent communist in all the villages in Samariya, calls me "Uzik Mujik." I asked around about the word "mujik," and when I heard it means "farmer" in Russian, I thought it was a perfect nickname for someone who lives in an agricultural village and makes his living keeping bees. It even sounded to me like a compliment. Then, I found out that the Russian word has another meaning—"ignoramus"—and that sounded pretty insulting to me. Like the "analphabet" Zionka's mother and Mali Perlmutter, the watchmaker's wife, shout at me. Every time I'm in the bakery, I try to figure out from Aharonchik's voice whether he says "Mujik" out of affection, or whether he means to hurt me, and that's not easy to do, because a person's voice sometimes sounds one way, and sometimes another.

The simplest things in Aharonchik's place, "Half a bread" or "Two Sabbath challahs" sound like a speech. After he finishes off three vodkas, he starts calling me *tovarish*—"friend" in Russian—and when he begins singing about great Mother Russia, I wait for him to call me an "anarchist."

Even if Aharonchik planned to announce to the entire world that I was an illiterate ignoramus, I couldn't argue with him, because it was true. I still hadn't learned how to read, and my teachers had given up on me. When they wrote on the board, the only thing I could do was listen to the squeaking of the chalk, and the letters looked to me like scared insects. I would look at the other kids' bent heads and my eyes would immediately fall on Zionka's golden hair. They'd all be writing away, and I didn't understand what I was doing there and why I wasn't outside. I once tried to copy from the board, but when I looked away for only a second, I couldn't find the word again. The letters had just disappeared.

A long time ago, I asked Aharonchik what the word "anarchist" means. He grinned from ear to ear and even gave me a fresh roll, hot from the oven. "A lawbreaker. Someone who doesn't accept the rules and lives in complete freedom," he said, and that was the biggest compliment I ever got in my life.

I don't even have any notebooks, just books that I never open, and it's only out of "the goodness of her heart," as my teacher said, that I am tested orally. Every year, they threaten to keep me down, but I manage to pass the tests at the last minute.

They say, "Nothing will ever come of him, the poor orphan, a wild, neglected little devil." They don't even bother to whisper or talk behind my back, as if I were deaf too, and everyone admires Aunt Miriam for agreeing to look after me and taking on such a heavy burden.

She says, "An obligation is an obligation" and "Blood is thicker than water," a smug expression spreading across her face. The village rabbi comes to visit us once a week, drinks tea in the china cups with the flower design that Aunt Miriam takes out of the sideboard especially for him, and listens patiently to all her troubles. He compliments her when he arrives, "Who can find a woman of valor," and before he leaves, he puts his hand on my wild hair and says, "A blessing on your head. The Almighty, blessed be His name, is a great prankster, like you," and then he kisses the mezuzah.

Only two people in the entire village—the rabbi and the principal—call me by my real name, Uziel, the name my father gave me the day I was born. To this day, Imri claims he chose the name, but I don't believe him.

I once heard Zionka's mother warn her not be my friend, because I'm a pest and bigger troublemaker than the British, and that was a real insult, because the English rule Palestine and don't allow us to call it our homeland. Even Mohammed Daudi hates them, and he says, "With God's help, one day they'll leave here with their tail between their legs."

But I actually secretly admire their spick-and-span uniforms and pilots' hats, but can't say so openly. Whenever they practice marching in formation with their hobnailed shoes clacking rhythmically, and they come close to our land where the beehives are, I untie Johnny Weissmuller, my dog, to scare them. But even if they are scared, it's hard to tell. They go right on marching in perfect step, maybe because the pilot observing them, an officer with light-colored hair and a neatly trimmed mustache, is more of a threat to them than my dog.

I didn't play any serious pranks all those months that Imri was away from home. Except for the time I jumped through the window of the village committee house, disrupting a lecture being given by one of the leaders of the Jewish community on the situation in the country. I fell inside at exactly the moment he was talking about Lord Passfield's White Paper, a document that stated how many new immigrants were allowed to come to Palestine and that no one could come near it without a paper known as a "certificate." Papers were my enemy, I explained to Zionka. Especially what was written on them. I don't see the words, only the white spaces between them, and sometimes, I try to read them instead of the black marks.

I landed exactly when they were arguing about whether the letter sent by the English Prime Minister, McDonald, to Chaim Weizmann would remedy the situation. Aharonchik the baker argued fervently that it was just another English swindle. The lecturer, an important person who had come especially from Tel Aviv, smiled at me as I landed on his table, and proclaimed, "Here's a sign from heaven! This is the child for whose sake we are struggling," and while I was still trying to get down off the table, I said to the audience that I was not willing to be anything for the sake of anybody. My teacher, who was also present, suggested sending me as a gift to the English in exchange for a few new immigrants.

And there was one more small prank. I sent Johnny Weissmuller to chase the ducks in Zionka's yard. I was lucky that Zionka burst out laughing when she heard the chorus of quacking and didn't snitch on me to her mother, who would've sent me straight to Aunt Miriam, because Zionka's mother thought I was a hopeless case. But Zionka's father actually liked me, and every weekend, when he came home from paving roads, he wanted to know what pranks he'd missed, and he would burst out laughing and say, "This is the new generation of Jews that aren't afraid of anything." The words didn't comfort me, because Zionka's father didn't have the slightest idea what I really was afraid of.

I followed Imri's instructions, and I did all the jobs Aunt Miriam assigned me. Mohammed and I harvested the honey, and he didn't let me do too much licking. He said we have to leave room on our tongue for the taste of onions too.

Aunt Miriam continued to complain that the burden—namely, me—was pushing her poor shoulders down to the ground, and what a tragedy had befallen her when my parents were taken and she was left with the responsibility, and who knows what was in store for all of us in this crazy country. I sometimes thought she was mad at my father because his heart suddenly stopped beating without any warning, and I think to myself, the poor man, why does he have to be blamed for dying? Aunt Miriam never had any complaints about my mother, and maybe that's because my aunt loved her younger sister very much, and didn't actually believe she was dead. Every day, she talked to her in the empty air, usually when her hands were busy shining the Sabbath candlesticks. She reported to her on how many centimeters I'd grown, she lied about my progress in reading, and she also told her how many new immigrants over the quota had sneaked into the country, right under the nose of the English. Everything Aunt Miriam told my mother sounded better than it was in reality, maybe so the woman in the air wouldn't worry and think the situation had gotten worse since she left us.

Sometimes Aunt Miriam would take a break between the things she was saying, as if she were listening to replies. She'd be so quiet and absorbed that I was sure my mother was answering her. I tried to talk to my mother in the air too, but for me, the air always stayed empty.

The morning after Imri left, Aunt Miriam devoted

most of her conversation with my mother to a detailed description of her older son's important mission, finishing up with the sentence that always ended those conversations, "I hope you are well where you are." Then Aunt Miriam put the shining candlesticks back on the shelf that held all our religious objects. The rabbi always marveled at the "heavenly glow" that came from them.

I didn't know how long Imri would stay away. Did getting married take a long or a short time? And maybe he'd want to stay in Europe, which was so beautiful and peaceful. I hoped he'd come back. Aunt Miriam had no doubt that he would, but I wasn't completely sure.

Time is something I think about a lot, especially since the day I went to the movies.

Chapter 3

Four months passed. I didn't know if that was considered a long or a short time. For me, it was an endless period of time, cut into slices of ordinary events of the kind we don't pay attention to. We received one postcard, and aunt Miriam read it out loud. Imri told us not to worry about him, described the gorgeous European countryside, and said how sorry he was that he didn't have a camera to immortalize everything. He didn't mention the new bride. The back of the postcard showed the watercolor drawing of a small village, something like our own village, except that white snow covered the slanted roofs of the houses, and there was a cross at the top of the church.

There had already been a succession of three or four queens in our hives, and only the taste of the honey stayed the same. Mohammed Daudi went all the way to Gaza with his hives for the nectar from the cactus flowers, and had already returned. New chicks had hatched from the eggs in the hen house, and the ducks in Zionka's yard had already learned to swim in the washtub. It is impossible to skip over even the smallest things. What happens is what's supposed to happen, the rabbi says, but I don't agree with him. If he's really the blessed Almighty's representative on earth, why doesn't he have a few words with his boss and explain to Him that it's all so boring if we know everything beforehand. In one of her daily conversations with my mother in the air, Aunt Miriam told her that Imri and his bride would be coming home soon.

I was surprised. Why should the bride come back home with Imri? Aunt Miriam told me specifically that she wasn't a real bride. Imri didn't even know his new wife, that's what I told Zionka. Like a true expert, I said, "You see, Zionka, they made them a couple only to trick the English. It's a 'fictitious' marriage, Zionka. That's a word you have to remember, 'fictitious.' You don't have to know how to write it." And I also told her—word for word from the mouth of Aharonchik the baker, "The reason our best boys volunteer to marry Jewish girls they don't know in Europe is to have their names entered in their passports as their legal wives, and to avoid having to get a 'certificate,' without which, you can't get near this country." It all sounded like the kind of really clever prank I'd love to take part in.

Zionka was less enthusiastic than I was. She shrugged and said, "I wouldn't agree to marry just any boy who all of a sudden arrived from Palestine. That bride probably didn't even know the difference between the Eretz Israel in books and the real Palestine here."

Then I told her what I'd told my teacher, "You don't understand, Zionka. It's all for the sake of the homeland."

One of the ducks quacked, as if backing up what I had said. It was the duck we later called "the Zionist duck," because it loved to peck at the picture of Herzl,

19

especially that sentence I don't know how to read, but can say perfectly, "If you will, it is no fairy-tale."

And I even boasted to Zionka, "When I grow up, I'll volunteer too. I'll even agree to get married a hundred times, until we have our own country." But I only said that to impress her because, for Zionka, the homeland is no joke.

She said, "You know, Uzik, that woman will be your sister-in-law."

I rolled the new word around on my tongue and said, "I never had a sister-in-law."

Zionka warned me, "Be careful of her. Even a 'fictitious' sister-in-law can be a witch, like the stepmother in fairytales who throws the child out of the house." But somehow, I wasn't scared.

Aunt Miriam told my mother in the air that Imri was bringing his wife to live with us until she found her relatives. And just so my mother wouldn't worry, she added that, in the meantime, while Imri was staying in the country, the village rabbi would arrange a quick divorce, and then Imri could go back to Europe and marry a second bride. Aunt Miriam added, "You see, my sister, everything is under control."

It sounded complicated. Getting married "fictitiously," getting divorced "fictitiously." I thought it was a much more serious prank than any of mine, but it seemed that everything was allowed when it came to the homeland. Aunt Miriam assured my mother in the air that none of this was being done behind the rabbi's back. He was part of it. Aunt Miriam explained everything very seriously, and it was hard for me to understand how dead people could understand anything so complicated, because I don't believe there's a homeland in heaven.

I'm not sure I'm too crazy about the idea of a strange woman suddenly coming to live with us. If they tell me to leave my room, I won't do it. Everything is exactly where I want it to be, even if Aunt Miriam claims my room is a total mess, and even the blessed Almighty couldn't find His way in it. I don't like changes, I don't want to change, even though Zionka's mother thinks that's exactly what I need. I hope that Polish woman is a short-term guest.

Aunt Miriam said to the rabbi, "So, all right, another burden to bear, but I'm used to it already."

Aunt Miriam didn't close her mouth, making the room spin from so many words and china cups. She promised the rabbi she would do everything to help the poor girl until she could manage by herself in the country. A new immigrant with delicate hands who would complain about the heat and the mosquitoes and how hard it was to find a job. We'd have to explain to her that here, you have to work at all kinds of different jobs, and women even go out to work in the quarry, or go from house to house selling "laundry bluing" in small tin boxes. "We don't have any time here for idleness or recreation," Aunt Miriam proclaimed, as if recreation were a dangerous disease, and she bragged so much about our wonderful Imri, the precious son of the entire village, who was sacrificing his passport on the altar of the nation. He had promised the Jewish Agency to marry at least four women for them. She never called *him* a "burden."

The rabbi swallowed the hot tea in one gulp, as if the pale brew had suddenly been struck by frost, and said,

"They shall come to this land no matter how much the English, may their names be cursed, rant and rave," and for a minute, he reminded me of Mohammed Daudi.

Imri

You're an experienced man, Aharonchik, you've seen the world and you took part in the great revolution. How should I act with a woman? Do I flatter her, even if she isn't beautiful? And what do women in Europe wear? I hardly get any sleep, and all the fellows wink at me and roll their eyes, as if I'm about to enter the gates of heaven. I can't ask my Aunt Miriam or our next-door neighbor, Zionka's mother. The other women in our village wear shabby clothes that hide their bodies. I secretly opened my mother's closet to look inside, but then I lost my nerve. After all, my mother was born here, not in Europe. I remember one gray dress. She wore it the day she gave birth to my little brother. On that day, she was so heavy she could barely move, and only her smile shone. She took my little hand, and spreading the fingers, she placed it on her swollen belly, saying, "This is life."

Chapter 4

On the day Anna arrived, Johnny Weissmuller tore his leash and ran off to the English air force base. Instead of going to school, I went out to look for him in the village. The ducks in Zionka's yard were strolling around leisurely, so I understood the dog wasn't there. Zionka's mother came outside and ripped into me. "What are you doing here? Zionka is an outstanding pupil. Stop bothering her, you nincompoop."

I'd never been called that name before. Zionka's mother was original. Too bad Zionka's father only came home on the weekends. As for her mother, I thought, how generous her imagination is with words, but how stingy she is with her smiles.

The Zionist duck ran towards me, quacking loudly, and I'd already decided that it had a special fondness for people who didn't know how to read. Then it tried to get out onto the street, and Zionka's mother chased it inside with a stick, calling it a nincompoop too.

I went to Aharonchik's bakery. I was always looking for excuses to go there. He gave me a hot roll, and in exchange, I had to listen to one of his fiery speeches on the socialist revolution about to take place throughout the world. Always sticking out of the baker's pocket was the

Yiddish newspaper he received in the mail from Moscow once a month. That's where he got his information about the future, and he told everyone that it was the only newspaper that printed the truth, because that was its name. Aharonchik saw dangerous aristocrats and imperialists lurking in every corner, and he dreamed of a state filled with Jewish and Arab workers, who would live together in brotherhood and equality, raising high their red flag. Hanging over the oven was a picture of Stalin, an angry, mustached man, whom he called "the sun of all nations," even though that gloomy man looked to me like he actually liked the dark better.

"Have you seen Johnny Weissmuller, Aharonchik? He's not a communist. Just a plain old dog." But before I could get an answer, I first had to listen to a passage in Russian from the *Communist Manifesto* by Marx and Engels, which Aharonchik thought was the most important book ever written. I told him that written things can't be that important, and Aharonchik clutched his head and said, "Mujik, what's to become of you?"

Then I went to Meir the butcher, who is the most charming man in our village. Zionka's mother always stays in his shop longer than she has to just to buy a measly old chicken wing. I hoped Johnny Weissmuller, who was always hungry, was lying in wait there for a bone someone might generously decide to throw him, but the dog wasn't at the charming butcher's shop either.

I whistled for him, a perfect imitation of Tarzan's roar in the only movie I ever saw, when I went to Tel Aviv with Imri at the beginning of the summer. Thirty-one reels at the Beit Ha'am movie theater. Not a dilapidated old shack like the one in our village, but a real theater, with a flat white screen and wooden folding chairs, and an usher and a candy vendor who passed through the aisles with a box hanging around his neck on a strap, calling "Chocolate, mints, chewing gum." Every night, before I fell asleep, I rolled the pictures around in my memory. Sometimes, in the right order, and sometimes in a new order that I chose, and it didn't cost thirteen cents a ticket.

Johnny Weissmuller leaped from branch to branch, roaring as he hovered in the air, dropping down easily from African trees so huge, they hid the sky. What a sound came out of his mouth! Lying in bed, I covered my ears. Imri said it was just a trick they do in the movies, but I didn't believe him. I was positive it was Johnny Weissmuller's real voice.

I searched everywhere for sounds and listened to them. Since the movie, I was practicing feeling things through my ears. I could walk with my eyes closed and always know where I was. The kids playing stickball during recess, and the little ones in kindergarten singing off-key. The rabbi standing at the door of the synagogue with the sexton, trying to settle an argument between him and Alter, who owns a citrus grove, about how much to pay for being called up to read from the Torah. I also listened to the clanking of the milk pails in the dairy belonging to Altschuler, who brags that he doesn't dilute his milk with water, and the cases of beer being unloaded at the entrance to Shmariyahu's grocery, and I listened to the ticking of the clocks in the shop belonging to Ephraim Perlmutter, the watchmaker. His wife, Mali, always stops me at the door to the shop and asks me to do her a favor and give a message to her best friend, Zionka's mother.

I walked from one end of the village to the other, whistling and searching, until I reached our beehives. I leaned against the sealed boxes, wooden panels covered with gray-painted tin, my ears straining to hear the buzzing inside. Maybe hundreds, even thousands, of creatures lived inside, and no one in the world could tell them apart. Even the oldest, most experienced beekeeper doesn't expect to get a smile from a bee, because we don't understand bee jokes. Here, in the closed, not very large, box, every bee knows its job—the worker, the queen, the male—and Mohammed Daudi doesn't think they dream of being something else. "Bees," he explains, "never sleep, and that's why they don't have dreams." I learn everything from Mohammed, who's been working with bees for a very long time and knows how to identify the different kinds of honey according to the nectar they're made from, and has been to every far corner of the country, because he moves his hives from one place to another, depending on the season.

Suddenly, I heard Johnny Weissmuller barking. I bent down under the hive and started looking. For a minute, I was afraid he'd managed to open the cover and dive inside, and was now battling a whole swarm. But then I saw him running on the other side of the fence, inside the English pilots' base.

If I had known where he'd gotten in, how he'd crossed to the other side of the tall barbed wire fence and gotten past the sentry who sits at the entrance day and night, with his rifle in his hand, I would have followed him. I looked for a hole in the fence, but couldn't find one.

The camp was an island surrounded by signs. I knew that they warned, "Military property. No admittance!" even though I couldn't read them.

The parade grounds on the other side of the fence were empty. I had to save Johnny Weissmuller before some English pilot decided to make him a new immigrant in the opposite direction, and arrange an English "certificate" for him.

I dragged one of the hives carefully, so the bees wouldn't go wild. It was heavy, but I managed to move it closer to the fence so I could use it as a ladder. If Mohammed could see me now, he would be proud of my ingenuity, and I was just as strong as the real Johnny Weissmuller in "Tarzan, King of the Apes."

I climbed onto the gray box, careful not to shake it and upset the bees, and, watching out for the sharp points of the barbed wire, I jumped inside. Now I was standing in the middle of the parade grounds that were all shiny like Aunt Miriam's candlesticks. There were long Quonset huts among the pine and eucalyptus trees whose trunks had been freshly whitewashed. Curbstones and rope fences lined both sides of the paths. In the distance, I could see the stretch of flat red earth they used as a landing strip, and that too was marked with whitewashed stones.

The English base was silent. The midday sun was blazing, even though it was already autumn. Aunt Miriam says that this is the time of day when even God, blessed be His name, grabs a nap and forgets about everything. I understood why the English curse the weather in Palestine when they're buying their bottles of cold beer at Shmariyahu's grocery, losing their English politeness for a minute. Aharonchik watches them every day, and says that people who drink whisky instead of vodka will never rule the world.

Johnny Weissmuller had disappeared. I started to cross the grounds, my shadow in front of me. I walked past the big hangar where they repair airplanes and slowly approached the planes that were lined up on this side of the landing strip. I'd never seen an airplane close up. Its body was painted silver, and its tail was blue, white and red, like the circle imprinted on its side. The nose was yellow, and the machine gun protruded from behind the cockpit. I just had to touch the wings of the Hawker. Herzl Fleischer in my class would die of jealousy. Maybe he's an expert in weapons, but he never touched the wings of a real airplane.

Near the landing wheels of the last Hawker in the row, Johnny Weissmuller barked with happiness, as if he had just finished wolfing down all the salami in the English pilots' canteen. He wagged his tail, and I whistled a quiet Tarzan whistle at him.

Suddenly, a hand grabbed me.

"What're you doing here, kid?" someone asked me in English, shaking me by my collar. It was the pilot with the light-colored hair and the well-trimmed mustache who observed the soldiers marching. His shoes gleamed, and every button and buckle on his blue uniform glittered.

I understood every word. I also knew Russian from Aharonchik, I'd picked up Yiddish from the rabbi's conversations with Aunt Miriam, and I'd learned Arabic from Mohammed. But that didn't mean a thing to them. All they cared about was reading and writing. Too bad the words didn't get into my head through my eyes the way they did through my ears. They turned upside down on the page, twisted and turned like little worms, changed places and fell inside each other. Only in my ears did the words stop moving, and I understood them even when they were in a different language.

I stuttered. "I'm looking for someone."

"Anyone in particular?" the pilot asked.

"A friend."

The officer was tall. Much taller than I remembered when I saw him observing the obedient soldiers on the other side of the fence.

"We don't find friends easily. Perhaps someone sent you to sniff about here?"

"Sniff about?" Now I was scared. I felt so small next to him.

"Spy. Count the number of planes on the ground. Here, this is a Hawker. A two-seater bomber that pecks at you like a hawk."

"I'm looking for Johnny Weissmuller."

The pilot burst out laughing. Even his mustache shook.

"You won't find him. This isn't a Hollywood studio with an African set."

I felt myself starting to get angry. I didn't know where Hollywood was.

"There he is," I pointed to the dog barking happily near the plane's tail. "And besides, Tarzan is not a set. It's all real."

The pilot raised his hand and pointed, but I didn't know at what. The stripes on his sleeve glowed in the sun. Two blue ones on each side, and another two turquoise ones separated by a thin line as clear as air.

"You see, this is also a set. Nothing here is real."

Hollywood? Where is Hollywood? I didn't know any new immigrants who came from Hollywood. And maybe this Englishman had finished a case of beer and was just plain drunk. He signaled with his finger again, and Johnny Weissmuller jumped out from behind the tail of the plane and stood in front of him, like one of his obedient marching soldiers. The officer uttered something in a quiet voice, and the dog sat down, looking up at him expectantly. The pilot made another gesture with his hand, and Johnny Weissmuller began to follow him obediently, as if he'd always been his dog.

I said in a choked voice, "I wish you'd go away from here. This isn't your homeland."

"So I have a patriot here," the officer said, smiling. Johnny Weissmuller was still lying at his feet, waiting patiently for instructions. "Little Zionist, are you too hiding guns and learning how to shoot?"

"Patriot" was a word everybody used. There wasn't a single one of us who didn't think he was a patriot.

"Love of the homeland," the pilot laughed. "You'll discover one day that there are things one loves more."

I remembered what Mohammed once said about the British. "Someday, you'll leave here with your tail between your legs." And I added, "And you won't be wagging your tail anymore."

I thought the English pilot would hit me, but he

burst out laughing again. His mustache fluttered and the Hawker's wings shook as if it were a giant bee. A machine gun protruded from the machine-gunner's empty compartment.

"Go home, little Zionist, and don't forget. A movie is just a set. So says Major Charles Timothy Parker of the Royal Air Force, always at your command!" And then he saluted me.

I whistled as loud as I could. In the movie, Johnny Weissmuller fought with his enemies. He wasn't a man who knuckled under or ran away from danger. I pushed my clenched lips, positive that my piercing Tarzan whistle would wake even God, blessed be His name, from His nap.

Johnny Weissmuller turned around and walked towards me with obvious reluctance, his shadow next to mine and his tail wagging merrily, as if nothing had happened. To make him mad, I told him about the expert sent here three years ago by the Ministry for the English Colonies. That man, whose name I don't remember, decided that there was no room left in Palestine for even one more cat.

I wanted to yell at Johnny, to show him that there wasn't any room in the country for dogs either, but he ignored me.

"A movie is real and so are you!" I roared at Major Charles Timothy Parker. I was far enough away so he couldn't grab me, and the gate sentry holding his rifle was far behind me too. Too bad I didn't get to touch the wings of the Hawker.

I ran all the way back, Johnny Weissmuller barking

behind me, sure that it was just a game. And then I saw Zusia the wagoner's horse and wagon at the entrance to our house. The light had faded and the sun had vanished behind the English base. Imri helped her down, exactly like an English gentleman knowledgeable in etiquette, wearing Father's best English suit. Aunt Miriam was watching them silently.

I saw a tall, slender woman wearing a dark dress and a hat put one foot in the air and step hesitantly onto the ground.

Imri lingered; he could've let go of her hand, but kept on holding it. He said softly, "Welcome, Anna."

Aharonchik

The most beautiful hands in the world are a working woman's hands, blistered and sweaty. Endless dedication and patience have carved furrows in them, and every rough caress will raise gooseflesh on your body. Pushkin was wrong. He investigated and found that in all of Russia there were no more than three pairs of beautiful legs. And as for hands, a true proletarian will not fondle you. She will knead your flesh with the force of her hopes. In the days to come, you will both be equals with the same rights.

You, Imri, belong to a tough and stubborn generation, and you must prepare yourself for a life of toil to make this fallow land of thorns and sand fertile, so that it bears fruit. And the woman will choose you to share with her the rage and the joy. Her clothes will be plain, her throat exposed, her feet bare, and she will behave simply and candidly. Away with false manners and fancy clothes. Today, we'll strip off the fur of the past and stretch our limbs. Flesh and sun. We will shake off every oppressive burden, Imri, because property crumbles into dust and in the Hebrew future, a day will come when she'll turn to you and say "my man" and not "my husband."

I long now for a warm bosom. Talk to them, Imri, maybe they'll send me on a mission too. Someday I'll find a woman after my own heart. We'll sit in the open field under the reddening sky, and we'll unbutton every button of our shirts and cry out together, "Lovers of the world unite."

Chapter 5

Aunt Miriam went berserk. The whole village heard her shouting, because people had gradually been gathering on our street to get a look at the strange woman who had arrived and maybe also to secretly enjoy the punishment awaiting me. Zionka's mother was there too, like a policeman called to do his job, and the Zionist duck had followed her, taking advantage of the opportunity to escape from the permanent imprisonment she had condemned him to.

"I'm sick and tired of it!" Aunt Miriam shouted. "The principal told me he would expel you. Trouble is all you bring me. When will you ever give me some happiness?" She was practically crying.

Imri hugged me, looking all the while to see Anna's reaction. I wasn't sure he hugged me just because he'd missed me.

"You were waiting for us, right? He just wanted to welcome Anna and me, Aunt Miriam. This is the last time he'll play hooky from school. He promises, don't you promise, Uzik?"

Anna didn't say a word. She still hadn't taken off her wide-brimmed hat. I looked her over secretly and didn't promise a thing. Promises are false, and I don't even know how you tell the difference between a real bride and a "fictitious" one.

Aunt Miriam talked to her for the first time.

"*A tachsheet*," she said in apology, calling me another Yiddish name that could be added to the growing list, and she still hadn't introduced me to Anna.

"Now you're going to stay in your room without going out for three days, do you hear?"

Imri's pleading didn't help, and Zionka's mother glowed with victory, encouraging Aunt Miriam to think she'd done the right thing, because "a firm hand is required here." And a slap would've have been fine too, because back in Poland, they used a belt to beat smart-alecks like me. If the rabbi had been there, he would definitely have convinced Aunt Miriam to lighten the heavy punishment, but he was at evening prayers at that hour.

Anna still hadn't spoken. I had no idea what kind of voice she had and what language she spoke. It was too bad she wasn't standing next to me. Then I would've had a chance. Aunt Miriam always wanted strangers to know that we were a decent family, and in spite of all our tragedies, we were all good people who obeyed the law and the commandments.

Imri tried to console me, "Don't worry. I'll soften her up." He dragged Anna's valise inside, and then pulled in a heavy trunk. The latch opened and the cover rose to reveal embroidered pillows, bundles of clothes and underwear, and even a fur coat, which worried me a little, because I thought she would be leaving before winter came. And anyway, who needs a fur coat here?

Johnny Weissmuller sniffed the trunk and then Anna. She had a flowery scent I'd never smelled before, the smell of a nectar that our bees had never come across either. She bent down, patted the dog's head, still not saying a word. I calmed down. Silent new immigrants wouldn't cause trouble in Eretz Israel where people talk too much and everything is done with a lot of noise, as Aharonchik the baker says.

Imri was dressed up like a bridegroom. Now I noticed that my father's best suit was shabby and the sleeves were too short. Imri's sunburned hands stuck out of the white cuffs, and he didn't seem to know what to do with them. His tie was actually tied tightly to his collar, firm and neat. Maybe the bride had finally taught him how to tie it. It was too bad that I missed seeing Imri break the glass. I would've put a wrapped-up stone under his foot, and that prank would've turned the wedding into a wild celebration. Even when Imri was talking to Aunt Miriam, his eyes were fixed on Anna, following every small movement she made.

"I touched the wings of a real Hawker today," I said, pulling my brother's sleeve, but this important piece of news didn't make him take his eyes off Anna. Johnny Weissmuller stayed at her side too. Today, he preferred strangers. An English pilot and a Polish bride on the same day was too much for me. I turned around and started walking towards my room on the top floor. A fake bride. Why did they have to stick her in our house? Let her relatives take her. I hoped the next bride Imri brought for the homeland would be different. This is the first one, I said to myself as I locked my door from the inside. He'll do better the next time.

Johnny Weissmuller barked and scratched at the door, but I didn't open it.

Having to stay in my room for three days was unfair punishment.

The things they did to me were the things they hated other people to do to them. They cursed the English for locking them in their houses after a little incident on the road, but that didn't keep them from punishing me by keeping me under house arrest. I kept repeating, "You yourselves are English!" and felt I was getting stronger.

From my window, I watched Anna walking around the yard with Johnny Weissmuller. She didn't go out into the main street. Sometimes, she threw a branch or a leaf, and Johnny would dash off and bring it back to her, wrap himself around her feet and gurgle with pleasure, like a child who's made his mother happy. While Zionka's mother was doing the laundry in a tub, she sometimes looked to see what was happening in our yard. I opened my mouth wide and showed my teeth, trying to imitate Johnny Weissmuller at his angriest, and Zionka's mother shook her fist at me.

Out of boredom, I started talking to myself. "*Ya'allah, ya'allah*," I said in Arabic, "Come on, let that Polish woman get out of here." Suddenly, I sounded like Mohammed. We can't tell anyone she's mute, because if her relatives find out, they won't want to take her. I took a shot at the collection box for the Jewish National Fund that was hanging on the wall.

I spent the first day full of expectations. I peeked out the window to see whether the rabbi had come yet to

39

divorce her from my big brother.

Imri disappeared. I pressed my ear against the closed door and listened. I didn't hear his footsteps, or the stupid songs he sang when he shaved. I admit I was disappointed that Imri forgot to bring me a present from Europe. The Polish woman scared me with her silence, and even though I knew that mute people were also deaf, I had a feeling she heard everything.

Aunt Miriam sent her to bring me food three times a day. She knocked very quietly at the door, and when I opened it, I found the tray on the floor and saw the hem of her dark dress disappearing down the hallway.

Once, I beat her to it. I opened the door wide, and she was still standing there. I said, "We don't want you here. The only reason Imri brought you is because he's a patriot." And I also informed her that Imri had promised the Jewish Agency he would marry at least four brides, and the sooner she left, the faster he would fulfill his duty to the homeland.

She put the tray slowly on the floor and bent her head. But I still managed to see her face. She wasn't beautiful. I thought that was best for all of us, because a beautiful bride could complicate things. The Polish woman had gray eyes. A strange color. I didn't even think there were eyes the same color as the smoke that comes out of the train to Haifa, or the color of a really cloudy day, when you're not sure it'll rain and in the end, you're disappointed. My mother had a dress that color, the one that was still hanging in the closet. I didn't think Aunt Miriam had ever worn it.

I picked up the tray. "And keep away from my dog.

Johnny Weissmuller bites if you make him mad."

And then the woman smiled. Chills went through my body. As if the top of the beehive had come off and a swarm had burst out all at once. I took a step backwards and the tray fell out of my hands. The bread and the tomato landed on the floor, and the glass container of yogurt tipped onto its side, but didn't break. I picked it all up with shaking hands, feeling that I myself was mute. I shoved the slice of bread into my mouth and chewed it quickly, and she was still smiling. There was something else on the tray. A crystal ball with a small village inside it, covered by a transparent liquid. There were houses with red roofs, pointed fir trees and a wolf with a long tail that looked like Johnny Weissmuller, and when I shook the ball, snow started falling inside it. Even though I didn't like the ball, I wanted to run and hug Imri. In the end, his duty to the homeland and his bride didn't make him forget his promise. He did bring me a present.

Chapter 6

The first night, I woke up to the sound of voices. I didn't know what had awakened me until I saw the unfamiliar van parked near our toolshed. The van's door was closed, but a shaft of pale light crept though the crack, signaling me to come down.

I remembered what Johnny Weissmuller did in such situations. I pulled out the rope I kept coiled under my bed, tied it to the window sill and climbed down. I kept myself from roaring.

I was on the ground in a flash, the castor bush rustled and I froze. Then, like a real spy, I silently approached the toolshed. They were whispering inside. I heard one fellow say to Imri, "So, did you have a taste of your nectar yet, beekeeper?"

I didn't know what they meant. Coming from the toolshed was the sound of metal striking metal. What were they doing in the middle of the night with the tools we used for removing honey?

A second fellow said, "A terrific deal. Thanks to the English. They arranged a trip abroad for you, and also a hive full of honey. Lick away, lick away, Imri."

A strange conversation. Why did they think men were bees? Maybe they'd had some beer to drink too? Don't they know that the male dies when it inseminates the queen. I'll never be that stupid.

The first fellow asked, "Do you think the English suspect?"

Imri replied, "The clerk at the English Consulate who registered us as man and wife was very friendly. He wished us a long life of happiness together, and hoped we would have many children, and even called the woman clerk from the other room to see what a lovely couple we were. They searched the whole consulate for a camera to commemorate the occasion.

The second fellow was interested. "Tell me, is she pretty?" Imri didn't answer. Again I heard iron striking iron.

They were busy and didn't talk any more, and I already wanted to go back to my room. Then I heard Imri say, "The English clerk knew a lot about Jews. When he entered Anna's name on my passport, he said, 'With you people, matches are made in heaven.' We wanted to be on our way. We had our train tickets to the port of Constanza, where we were supposed to sail on the ship *Polonia*. The clerk was looking for excuses to keep us there, as if he were waiting for something."

I felt that the first fellow was tense. The second one said, "You have to be careful," and Imri assured them that he had convinced the clerk. His performance had been perfect.

"How did you do it?" both fellows asked at the same time, and Imri replied, "I kissed her."

I climbed the rope with the speed of Cheetah, Tarzan's chimp. I fell onto my bed but couldn't fall asleep. I saw the queen bee flying off to her wedding journey on a blazing afternoon. She took off like an arrow, heading for a place the other bees wouldn't dare go to. Even in the blinding sun, I could see that she had a human face. The males gathered around her, excited, fluttering their wings and competing with one another, and poor Imri was the first to reach her and didn't know what was in store for him. I shouted soundlessly, "Watch out. I don't want a disaster to happen." The English pilot, Major Charles Timothy Parker, was chasing both of them in his silver Hawker, a ferocious hawk that swoops down from the sky without warning. I called out to Imri, "You'll die!" and I didn't know whether I was awake or sleeping.

———

Everything was gone in the morning. There was no van parked near the toolshed, and Aunt Miriam and Imri were talking in the next room, as if he had never gone away. They had to check the beehive, because she didn't trust Mohammed or me, and they had to go to Tel Aviv to sell the honey for a good price, and he shouldn't forget to tell the rabbi to come to our house after prayers. That was an encouraging sign that the divorce was close. I didn't see Anna, and Johnny Weissmuller didn't go out to roam around like he usually did.

Zionka had stretched a string from her window to mine, with an empty tin can tied to each end, and told me that was a trick that would allow us to talk to each other. Even a whisper of hers into the can would reach my ears, sharp and clear. They had already installed in the Committee House that magical device you could talk into to someone far away. Only the village big shots and the English generals had one. They said you could even talk with someone on the other side of the world, Africa, for example, but I didn't believe it.

The string was stretched tight, balanced on each side. Zionka astonished me. I didn't know she had a hidden talent for tricks, and I spent the morning trying to guess what they would call her when they caught her doing something they didn't like. I made up some nasty names, but they absolutely did not rhyme with hers. Out of sheer boredom I even tried to write them down, but the minute I touched a pencil, my head started to hurt and the letters went wild. It's lucky that Zionka didn't see that fiasco. I threw out the paper right away.

Zionka was right. The magical device worked. She explained to me that you have to say "hello" at the beginning of the conversation. The word sounded so English and so strange that we laughed. We heard each other perfectly, but for some reason—maybe because we were so excited—we only asked, "How are you?" and "Who's speaking?" As if you couldn't hold a real conversation if you didn't see the face of the person on the other end.

And I also thought that, maybe, with the help of that great invention, I could talk to my mother someday.

And to my father too.

———

Mohammed Daudi waved at me from outside and shouted, "*Inshallah*, with God's help, everything will be all right." On the tray near the door, I found fresh pita that his sister, Fahtma, had baked especially for me.

Mohammed was a true friend. Even though he was Imri's age, and he had lots of little brothers and a sister named Fahtma and a cousin named Imad, he always had time for me. And when he invited me to his village, we rode horses together. Behind his back, Aunt Miriam calls him "the goy." My aunt, like Zionka's mother and her friend Mali Perlmutter, was afraid of Arabs. The two friends said that the Arabs would do anything to get us out of the country, that they wanted to slaughter all of us and throw us into the sea, but that didn't bother me. Those were just words. There was no point in listening to them, and certainly not in writing them down. Try to understand, Aunt Miriam, Mohammed taught me to ride a horse and whisper soft words in its ear so it would gallop straight ahead and not throw me onto the ground. And don't tell the rabbi anymore that we should never believe the *goyim* and that they deserve severe punishment. "Loyalty and trust," Mohammed said, "those are the most important things." A horse needs to know that you're willing to sacrifice something especially dear to you for him. Your freedom, for example.

It's too bad they couldn't fly Johnny Weissmuller to Mohammed's village to take riding lessons from him. It was true that Johnny Weissmuller was the swimming champion of the world and had everything, but if he rode a horse, it would be easier for him to fight the pygmy tribes. Even though I only saw the movie once, I remember every scene, and Mohammed was learning everything he needed to know from my stories. He promised me that one day, he would go to Tel Aviv just to see the movie at the Beit Ha'am Cinema.

I couldn't sleep again at night. Maybe because I didn't go outside and didn't burn up any energy. In her conversations with my mother in the air, Aunt Miriam explained that it was hard to control children like me, and she was doing everything she could to point me in the right direction. She sounded apologetic when she told my mother in the air that I spent most of my time out of the house, but she never admitted her failure, to save my mother from more sorrow. I wasn't sure Aunt Miriam told her she'd kept me in the house for three days.

I tied my rope to the window again and slid down it. It was so easy. I remembered what the English pilot with the long name had said, and I kind of liked the idea of being a spy sniffing around. Johnny Weissmuller also checks out the territory before he decides on a plan of action.

The whole house was filled with Aunt Miriam's snoring. She sometimes sighed and talked in her sleep. I thought she was carrying on conversations with my father. I'd gotten used to her snoring a long time ago, but Anna was probably tossing and turning in bed, so I went past Imri's room. I guessed that even a "fictitiously" married couple sleeps together.

Imri's door was open, and I saw that he wasn't even home. I couldn't keep myself from peeking inside. Anna filled the whole bed, lying on her side and hugging one of the embroidered lace pillows she'd brought with her. Her dark dress was hanging on the back of the chair, flowing all the way to the floor, without a wrinkle. Next to the pillow was an open book, her hand almost riffling it. She reads books, I said to myself, another reason to keep away from her.

The cover of her trunk was open, and I started poking around in it. I didn't know what I was looking for. Again, the air was filled with the smell of strange flowers that neither the bees nor I knew. I guessed it was the nectar the two fellows had been talking about, even though I had no idea exactly how you taste the nectar of a person.

I was disappointed. There were no treasures in the trunk. Only lace clothes that were too delicate, an old clock and a few records. I smiled to myself. The only gramophone was in the Committee House. Zionka's mother and Mali Perlmutter danced to its music as if they'd been invited to a ball by the High Commissioner.

Two candlesticks were hidden on the bottom of the trunk, under the ridiculous brown fur coat. That was a prank I hadn't yet played. I took one candlestick and shoved it under my pajama top.

That's it, I said to myself with the confidence of a victor. Now the fictitious bride has to go back to Poland. She'll think she forgot one candlestick.

Anna didn't move on the bed. It would be interesting to know whether she was mute in her sleep, too. Her body was covered up to her neck, with only her face resting on the pillow. I decided once and for all that she wasn't beautiful, and that made me happy. With a bang, I closed the cover of the beehive that was inside me, and again it started to open, and the bees tried to break out.

Footsteps outside broke the silence. I retreated. Imri was coming back to the house. I couldn't decide whether to go outside to him. I wanted so much to be alone with him, the way I was the day we went to the movies. A straw mattress lay on the floor near the door. It was now clear to me that a fictitious couple didn't sleep together. Imri was coming inside. I ran up the stairs, taking one last look at Anna.

Bright light poured over her, and two thin, moist streaks glistened under the lashes of her closed eyes.

I was back in bed. Like Anna, I too pulled the blanket up to my neck and then up over my head, as if I were folding myself into a trench. All of a sudden, I was cold. Maybe Imri was cold now too. I said to myself—out loud, this time—that I didn't care about Anna crying. Even though I didn't remember when I had cried the last time. Even when my father's heart suddenly stopped beating, there hadn't been any tears.

It was completely dark in the trench under my blanket. No movie started or ended, and I slammed shut the cover of the beehive inside me.

Chapter 7

The knocks were like the pecking of a stubborn hawk. I threw off my blanket and jumped out of bed, covered in cold sweat. At first, I didn't know where I was. The dream vanished instantly. The room was flooded with light, as if it were the middle of the day.

The hand knocking at the door was emphatic and impatient.

"I'm coming, Aunt Miriam!" I dragged myself towards the door and opened it.

Anna stood facing me. Her hands were empty, and there was no tray on the floor. She was wearing the dark dress that had been hanging on the back of the chair at night, and she looked straight into my eyes. Again, chills passed through my body.

"You can come out," she said, "your punishment is over."

Anna's voice was clear, even sharp. She spoke Yiddish.

I was stunned. It was a miracle. The mute had suddenly opened her mouth and spoken. Maybe the missing candlestick had unlocked her tongue. Had she already discovered that her precious object had disappeared?

Out of embarrassment, I kept opening and closing the top button of my pajamas.

"You can talk?"

"Did you think nobody in Poland ever spoke?"

I stood on tiptoe. She was so tall. I suspected she was taller than Imri.

"In Eretz Israel, people never shut up either. You'll see. Aunt Miriam learned from the English to set a quota for punishment, like their quota for giving out certificates. She said three days, and I won't leave a minute before they're up."

"Your aunt thinks you've had enough punishment."

"You don't know me. I can even stay in my room for a whole week. And anyway, I hate to be pitied."

Anna shrugged. "Pride is a luxury."

I said gruffly, "How do you say 'show-off' in Polish? I bet you have nasty names there too."

Anna said, "At school, they called me '*Żydowica*'," and then she looked into my room. It was a mess. Socks in every corner. I can never find a pair that matches.

"I don't think you're a show-off," Anna said. "Maybe a coward."

She'd probably found out that one candlestick was missing. I'd hidden it under my bed, together with my coiled Tarzan rope. Aunt Miriam yelled from the kitchen, "Troublemaker, even though you didn't apologize, I forgive you. Come downstairs."

Anna didn't come into my room, she just looked it over. A long, long time ago, when my mother was a girl, this had been her room.

Anna finally said, "There are cowards even in Palestine. Just as there's a shortage of courage in Poland."

I stood in the doorway and said bluntly, "So maybe

51

the English are right not to let you come here."

There was a blue collection box for the Jewish National Fund hanging on the door, and every Friday I dropped a penny into it. It was crooked from all my attempts to use it for target practice, with the help of my socks.

"*Żydowica*' is a really insulting name, right?"

We were still standing in the doorway.

Anna thought for a long time. She took a coin out of the pocket of her dress and dropped it into the blue box. "At the university, they separated the Jewish students from the others. They sat us on the left side. The Polish students used to walk around carrying long sticks with razor blades on the top. They attacked every Jew who crossed their path. The Jews were not allowed to go to medical school. And I wanted so much to be a doctor."

Then neither of us said anything. I thought for a minute that she was mute again. What would I do with a Polish coin? I didn't think the Jewish National Fund would accept it as a donation.

"You look so much like Imri." When she said his name, her lips looked like two arches and her cheeks glowed. If she'd met Meir, the charming butcher, first, my brother would never have had a chance.

The guys in the toolshed had talked about honey and the taste of heaven. I asked myself whether, when Zionka grew up, the taste of nectar would be in her mouth, and maybe in another place, too.

"You're the first bride." I stamped my foot to emphasize the warning. "There'll be three more after you." It didn't scare her, and she smiled as if she found me amusing.

I was bored the whole day. I didn't see anybody. I only heard Aunt Miriam's voice echoing through the house. This time, she wasn't holding any conversations with my mother in the air. She said to Anna, "Don't worry, Imri's looking for your relatives. He found out that they moved to Tel Aviv. He'll find them. You won't be alone."

I thought Imri was avoiding me. I hadn't been alone with him since he came back. He came in for a minute and went right out again, and then he came in again and went out again, so secretive. He whispered with the guys in the van, the ones who'd waited for him at night near the toolshed, and he didn't call me down even once. They gave two short beeps with the horn and he disappeared immediately. I didn't like strangers who messed up the order of things, and all of a sudden, I felt like Aunt Miriam when she gets mad at my father, who went and died without any warning. And the present I got made me mad too. Fake snow was all right for girls, maybe. If Zionka finally managed to teach me to write something, I'd give her the crystal ball as a gift, without letting Imri know.

Later, Aunt Miriam and Anna walked from the house in the direction of the synagogue and didn't come back until late in the afternoon, and again, there was a tray at my door with a slice of bread, a tomato and a glass of milk on it. But Anna didn't knock and didn't ask to come in.

I hadn't seen Mohammed all day, and Johnny Weissmuller preferred wandering around somewhere near the fence of the English air force base. I already regretted not accepting Aunt Miriam's generous offer of an early release. But honor, as Mohammed says, is also something worth fighting for.

I sat at the window next to the string Zionka had stretched between our windows, talking into the empty tin can, but no one answered from the other end.

———

In the morning, I organized my school bag. I put in the books I never opened and left early. Aunt Miriam was surprised, because I'm known for always being late to school. Everyone in my class thought I'd been sick and my teacher even asked how I felt, but I didn't believe he was really interested. You could see he was worried, because there was nothing written on the board. Zionka looked down and didn't say a word about my punishment, not even to Herzl Fleischer, the boy that all the girls liked, who passed her notes from the end of the row every lesson.

No one showed much of an interest in me. Everyone was excited. They said the English had started looking for weapons, that they suspected we were hiding rifles in the village. In the morning, soldiers had checked all the crates of beer in Shmariyahu's grocery, had searched the ovens in Aharonchik's bakery and dug around in the tubs of dough, and they'd stopped Zusia the wagon driver near the pine tree and examined every sack. They even demanded to come into the synagogue, but the rabbi blocked the door with his body, shouting at the soldiers, "The wicked shall have no hope."

At home, I found Anna in the kitchen, peeling potatoes. Her head was bent and the peels were dropping from the knife like twisted branches in the jungle. There was a piece of paper under the big pot. I could see right away that it was what Aunt Miriam called "a document." They thought pieces of paper were extremely important. They signed them and took vows about the future, and those were the pieces of paper people read or wrote that I hated the most.

Aunt Miriam and Anna stopped talking when I came into the room.

Aunt Miriam informed me that, "Starting tomorrow, Anna will help you with the beehives."

I understood from that that Anna was staying, and Aunt Miriam, as if she could read my mind, added, "For the time being."

In the evening, Anna and Imri sat on the porch. I was running after Johnny Weissmuller, teaching him how to run in circles. He'd started sucking up to me the minute my punishment was over. At first, I was tough with him, but it was hard to be too mad at a dog. I asked Johnny Weissmuller to show me how he managed to slip into the English base, and he wagged his tail, signaling that he was ready to take me there immediately, but it was already dark.

I didn't care if I was bothering Anna and Imri. I still hoped he'd pay some attention to me, that he'd say something to me, even ask how my reading was coming along, but they were caught up in each other, and I was as invisible as the air for them.

"The sky looks closer here," Anna remarked. I looked up to check, and it looked perfectly normal to me. Maybe only pilots see it differently. I didn't understand how a person could one day just leave the place he was born, the place he's so used to, whose language he speaks, and move far away to a place where, even if they beg him to come and promise him he'll be one of them, they keep on treating him like a foreigner. If they ordered me to live in the world that's inside the crystal ball, I would run away to Africa. If Imri hadn't been so busy working for the homeland, maybe he'd find out what I like more and what I like less. Sometimes, I thought he didn't know me at all, and I really didn't know him either.

Imri smoked cigarettes. Players. I'd already snatched a few from him and smoked them secretly in the toolshed and out where the beehives were. Only Johnny Weissmuller knew, but dogs never snitch. Sometimes, Imri smoked a pipe, but I didn't dare steal it, because he would know.

The burning red tip of his cigarette moved towards Anna. Through the curls of smoke, Imri said he didn't want to go, but he had to. He had no choice, because he had to do what he had to do. The day would come —

Johnny Weissmuller barked.

"Shut up," I scolded him, "and let me listen." I could hear better through the empty tin cans tied to the string.

I didn't know which one of them was taller. I think Anna was. Imri whispered, "These are just words on papers. They don't mean anything." Anna turned her head, looked again at the sky she thought was so close.

Imri touched her and asked her to wait.

Anna said, "It took us a week to get married in Poland. In Eretz Israel, it took me a minute to give you a divorce." Their heads were very close together. You couldn't see any separation between them. I couldn't tell whether, at that moment, he was tasting her nectar.

I whispered to Johnny Weissmuller that they were divorced. It was all over. Soon, she'd leave. The piece of paper on the table—not an especially big piece, just a few lines—was proof that now Anna was nothing to me. Not even fictitiously.

Chapter 8

Imri went to Europe for the second time and Anna gradually became part of the village. In the beginning, people would stop her on the street, or in Shmariyahu's grocery, and ask her where she was from, Warsaw or Galicia, Chelm or Lublin, Pinsk or Minsk, so the strange names of those places got stuck in my ears.

The ones who remembered Polish spoke Polish to her, and the ones whose father or grandmother was born there, before our village was founded, asked her if, by chance, she knew this man or that family, and they were very disappointed when she didn't.

They tried all kinds of accents on her, to see exactly what region she came from, and Mali Perlmutter whispered that she looked like a *shiksa*—a nasty name for a woman who isn't Jewish—and suggested the possibility that Anna was a spy the English had planted in the village to find out whether we were hiding weapons.

Zionka's mother also had relatives in Poland, who invited her to come with Zionka for the summer. In her high, squeaky voice, she questioned Anna about whether she should go. "How could it be that you never heard of the Rosenbergs? They have a lace and velvet factory and two stores on the main street of Warsaw." She bragged that her uncle ran a business patronized by aristocrats, and all the Polish ladies stood in line in his store to buy silk for their ball gowns. Then, Zionka's mother told everyone that Anna came from a *shtetl*, a remote little town on the Russian border that wasn't even on the map. In order to get out of that far-off place, where she didn't have a chance to get ahead, she latched onto the first man she could, our Imri. Some bargain.

And Zionka's mother said to the rabbi, "They should bring the Jews from Warsaw. They're a different class of people." And he said, "They are all our people. Many will come yet from the four corners of the earth. The ten lost tribes, even from Africa."

The rabbi drank tea at our house on his regular day. Sometimes, Aunt Miriam served herring, which I really hate. This time, Zionka's mother joined them. Like always, she said how beautiful the china was, and didn't forget to remind the people present that Aunt Miriam had inherited it from my mother. What interested her most was what Anna had brought with her from Poland. She'd sniffed out what was in the "dowry trunk," and she winked at my aunt when she called it that.

I said to the rabbi, "How will you know whether the people who come from Africa are Jews? Will you ask whether they're called 'dirty Jews' in Swahili?

Aunt Miriam wrung her hands. "What will I do with that boy? Only trouble he brings. All day long, he listens to the grown-ups' conversations. Don't you have anything to do, you little smart-aleck? Why don't you open a book? You don't try hard enough. You have to try."

Zionka's mother added, "What's that string between

our windows? Did you and Zionka decide to hang some Englishman on it?"

"It's our magical device, like the kind all our great leaders have, " I said. "A famous invention. You can talk to someone who's far away, someone you can't see."

The rabbi said, "We'll soon be sending messages to the Almighty Himself, may His name be blessed."

Aunt Miriam added another spoonful of sugar to her tea, stirring it over and over again. "He doesn't hear. You're better off talking to the air," she whispered, and I moved away from them.

Don't they have any nasty names for that Almighty they talk about as if He were a man? If we were created in His image, then it can't be that no one insults or curses him. I can't make up my mind whether to ask the rabbi. And another thought worries me. I really hope God can't read or write.

The three people in the room gulped down their tea in one swallow and complimented Aunt Miriam on her apple cake, the one they asked her to bake especially for all the weddings and bar mitzvahs in the village. The rabbi lowered his voice. "The English suspect," he said. "We have to be very careful. I told Imri he shouldn't rush to get married again, because the villains are checking every passport entry, and as far as weapons are concerned ..." and the rabbi stopped talking when he saw that I was devouring every word.

Anna was working in the hen house then. Aunt Miriam had taught her everything she needed to know about chickens. She got up early, gathered the eggs and waited for Zusia the wagon driver, who picks up the eggs from all the hen houses and brings them to Tnuva, the cooperative dairy. She also fed the chickens sorghum grains and made sure the chicks didn't escape from the coop. I said soft words to the chickens, the ones I learned from Mohammed to whisper in the horse's ear. I was sure Aunt Miriam hadn't taught Anna any soft words, because she said that talking to animals is a waste of time. You'd think talking to dead people made more sense.

Working with the beehives was more complicated. I felt experienced and important explaining to Anna everything Mohammed had taught me.

We were sitting in the toolshed, and I was taking apart the equipment and describing how the hive was built, where the queen bee's cell was, how the workers feed the female bee with special food that will turn her into a queen. And I also told Anna about the bees' special language, which is a language of dance. Sometimes they dance the "circle dance" and sometimes the "moving tail dance," and through their dancing, they tell the pollen gatherers where they should fly and where they can find the richest pollen. And while I was telling her, I kept looking at her lips.

At first, she remained standing. Maybe she thought it would be a short lesson. But when she became convinced that the words weren't coming to an end so fast, she knelt next to me, looking in amazement at the way I had folded my legs under me.

I said, "Try it, it's very comfortable," and continued explaining the signs, also using my hands, a language anybody could understand. When the honey is gathered, in the spring and summer, the bees are active, but in the autumn and winter, the hives are still. The bees huddle around the queen to protect her until the cold passes. And I told her that every hive has only one queen, and if, God forbid, another one suddenly appeared, the two would go to war. A queen would never draw her weapon, a crooked sword, from its sheath to use on a person, an animal or an ordinary bee, but only to fight an equal to the bitter end.

"The bitter end?" Anna sounded worried. She tried to fold her legs under her, like mine, but she couldn't manage it, because her long dress was in the way. She listened to me, like the best pupil in the class. She reminded me of Zionka. I showed her the tools we use for gathering the honey, the jars and the slabs of beeswax and the forks, and said, "Until one of them dies."

The toolshed was neatly organized. I suddenly had the feeling that it was too neat. I didn't remember that Mohammed or I had cleaned everything and put it all in its place like the English soldiers on the parade grounds. Even my grandfather's old clay pots, the ones he raised bees in in the old days, were leaning against the wall, and someone had wiped off the wax and the dust. I thought that maybe Imri had a guilty conscience for leaving me before the harvest season, and to make up for it, he'd prepared a surprise for us. All of a sudden, I noticed that something was missing. The old hives with the empty honeycombs we used only in the busy season, had disappeared. I didn't even have to move things around and look for them, because everything was standing there, except for the gray boxes.

Maybe Mohammed had taken them to his village to

fix or paint them, even though I didn't recall anything breaking.

Anna was running her fingers over the cells of the hive. For a minute, I suspected that she was the one who'd stolen the hives to get back at me for the candlestick I'd snatched.

"What do you do if the bees try to sting you?"

I said, "You stand still as a statue. Bees only sting when they feel something is threatening their lives, a hawk, for example. You don't move, and you breathe as quietly as you can. Till the danger passes."

"But you don't always know when the danger has passed." Anna pushed her hands into the protective gloves. "The bees see us differently than we really are, don't you think?"

I know everything about bees, Anna, even though they're always in motion, I can see them, I understand.

"They see different colors, nothing like the range of colors we see," I declared confidently. Maybe what we are isn't really what we are, and only the bees are smart enough to know that. They can't tell the difference between somebody from our village and somebody from an Arab village, or somebody from a *shtetl* in Poland, or from England.

Anna was putting on her beekeeper's mask. Her lips, with or without nectar, disappeared like the old hives. I heard her whisper, "I'm scared."

I realized then that Anna had not plotted to steal any hives. She didn't even know they existed. I stood up. For a minute, I was taller than she was. She was sitting at my feet, her legs folded perfectly under her.

Chapter 9

We worked quietly. Anna watched what I did and imitated me exactly. She learned fast and worked quickly. She sometimes looked curiously at the English base on the other side of the fence. One of the Hawkers took off and moved rapidly out over the sea. I asked myself whether I would ever get to fly.

Using long forks, we took off the coating of wax and put the slabs of honey inside the centrifuge. I turned the handle, and the honey poured out into the containers. Our bees are very good producers, Anna, and their honey is famous in the whole country. People order their autumn *Rosh HaShana* supply at Passover, in the spring. I don't have to read the labels I paste onto the jars. I've heard Imri repeat a thousand times that they say, "The First Hebrew Honey after Two Thousand Years. Made in Eretz Israel." I even remember my father reading the first label that came from the printers. It was a few days before his heart stopped beating.

Anna held the pouring device firmly. She had long, strong fingers, and she didn't let a drop of honey get away. Even though she was covered from head to toe, I could feel the fear oozing out of her. I worked without a mask, so she would know I wasn't afraid of any bee.

Deep down inside me, I was positive they recognized the troublemaker and wouldn't do him any harm.

"Is '*Żydowica*' worse than 'troublemaker'?" We were standing next to the English fence.

Anna didn't have a chance to reply.

"Here's our little Zionist spy," a voice came from the other side of the fence. "Where's Johnny Weissmuller?"

The English pilot, Major Charles Timothy Parker, was bent over, picking though the dirt, looking for something under the fence posts, and the horse standing next to him was trying to sniff the grass on our side. The Englishman straightened up. His brass buttons gleamed in the light of the setting sun.

"Is your Arab with you, too?" he asked, looking at the completely covered figure beside me. You couldn't tell it was a woman.

"Mohammed is not 'my Arab'. He's my friend!"

The sound of the airplanes had already been swallowed up by the soft darkness. The gliding Hawker left no traces in the sky.

"An Arab and a Zionist are friends? Palestine is a mad place."

"This is my brother's wife. My sister-in-law." First I said the word in English, then in Hebrew, even though it was a complete lie, because Anna wasn't anything to me anymore. I'd try to write the word sometime. It was so important to them that I know how to read and write, but the words always decided to run away from me. I had a feeling it happened to them too, sometimes, but they just wouldn't admit it. They said, "You are sanctified unto me," and then, "You are divorced from me." They wrote on the document, signed it—and in between, there was nothing.

Anna took off her mask. Her hair tumbled down. Red sun glowed on her lips.

The pilot inserted his forearm, covered with the stripes of his rank, through the wire lattice of the fence, avoiding the barbs.

"A pleasure to meet you. My name is Charles Timothy Parker."

She answered him simply, "I am Anna." Without mentioning her last name. She spoke English, and I was surprised to discover that, like me, she collected languages.

"You're new here," the pilot said—he didn't ask. Even though his voice sounded innocent enough, I suddenly realized that the ones on the other side of the fence were spying on us too. It was possible that they knew every one of us, and we'd never even noticed.

"Where are you from?" the Englishman asked.

"Poland."

"A lovely place. The heart of Europe. How did you become acquainted with your husband? I thought you Jews believe that matches are made in heaven." I didn't like the fact that he was questioning her. Even though Anna had admitted to me that she was a coward, she answered him easily.

"He came to visit relatives in my town. Lutsk. Have you heard of it?"

The Englishman shook his head.

"Is it a godforsaken little place like this one?"

Anna said, "He came to my parents' house to give

them a letter, and I knew right away."

It was incredible, the way she lied. The lies just rolled off her tongue. Maybe the Jewish Agency had ordered her to break all the Ten Commandments for the sake of the homeland. I convinced myself that I'd swiped the candlestick for the sake of the homeland too—and that is definitely not called stealing, I only did it so Imri would divorce her quickly and be free to fulfill his duty to marry four brides.

"Why leave Europe?" the pilot asked. "And of all possible places, why do they insist on this one? A wretched desert, no water. Even the green here has the color of a tubercular patient. Look." He pulled up a handful of grass from under the horse's bridle and handed it to her as if it were a bouquet of flowers.

"Do you know how to ride?"

"No." Anna didn't touch his fake bouquet.

The Englishman got onto his horse. He was wearing spurs. He looked down at her, still holding the handful of grass.

"I miss having a civilized conversation with someone. I've been stuck in this place for three years. Go back to Europe. Believe me. Your homeland has no future. Take your husband, or whoever, back to your Lutsk, build yourselves a nice house with a red tiled roof. Sit down to drink tea with milk at five o'clock, look out at the soft snow and listen to a Chopin polonaise. Your Moses lost his way. How could you not have understood that. And some other lunatic led the Arabs astray. What the hell are you trying to fix? You fled this place two thousand years ago and scattered throughout the world, and now you've gone mad and insist on returning."

Darkness had fallen. We couldn't really see him anymore. Only the silhouette of a man on a horse. I wanted Anna to answer him, to defend her Lutsk, or speak up for our village, but she only said, "Good night," with perfect English politeness, and put on her beekeeper's mask for no apparent reason. There was no danger lurking, because the bees don't look for pollen in the dark.

The English pilot approached the fence from his side, looking for a minute like a prisoner and, lowering his voice to a whisper, said, "I take off into the sky every day, and I've yet to see truly happy couples there. Sweet dreams, Annie. We shall meet again."

I was suddenly furious. At her, at the Englishman, at Imri who was devoted to the homeland and not to me, at Aunt Miriam, at my father who went and died without any warning, at my mother, who never answered when we talked to her in the air, and even at Johnny Weissmuller, who'd rather curl up at the feet of strangers.

The Englishmen struck at the horse's ribs. He was a good rider. The horse obeyed him. I saw how the Englishman bent over to whisper something in its ear, exactly the way Mohammed did. "Annie," he had called her. As if he'd known her for years. As if she were already half his own bride.

I shouted after him, "You just wait and see, Johnny Weissmuller'll show all of you," and I roared the famous roar.

We dragged the heavy tools that were covered with honey. I didn't even want to know how it tasted. I had a bitter taste in my mouth and my throat was dry from roaring.

Anna stopped halfway. She took off her mask and gloves and dipped a long finger into the honey. She licked it, and her lips glowed in the darkness.

She said, "Tarzan's real name is Lord Greystock. He was English."

I ran, bursting wildly into the toolshed, and threw the tools on the shelves and on the floor, panting. The place was a mess again. Now I felt comfortable. The toolshed was mine and Mohammed's, and I didn't need anybody to reorganize it.

I moved things, kicking at them. The old clay pots tilted over and fell. Suddenly, I saw a small door in the floor where they had stood. It had been hidden under the broken boards and hen house netting. I pulled the door, but it didn't budge. I pulled it again with all my strength, roaring, and I didn't care if Anna heard it and was scared. Finally, the little door opened, and I saw that our old hives had been squeezed into the black opening. I pulled one out. The hive was heavy, as if it were winter now and all the bees were gathered inside it to protect the queen from the invasion of strangers. Maybe this was where Aunt Miriam was hiding the *pfuntim,* the sterling she was saving up for my future.

I pressed my ear to the opening. Silence inside. Using one of the forks, I pushed away the burlap sack. I wasn't thinking about what would happen if the bees burst out all at once. I pushed my nose inside as far as it would go. I was hardly breathing. I smelled honey and wax and propolis mixed with something else, something like motor oil. I opened my eyes wide. On the bottom of the hive, under the slabs of wax, where the most dedicated workers live, I saw rows of guns lined up in perfect order.

Chapter 10

A hidden supply of guns at our place? Only watchmen and policemen who worked for the English were allowed to carry guns. That was the first secret I ever kept from Mohammed. My heart was heavy. I couldn't fall asleep. As if there were two Uziks, one on each end of a string stretched inside me, arguing. I hear them talking to each other through empty tin cans.

One Uzik said, shame on you. Mohammed is your best friend. He taught you everything you know. He always found time for you, and he never tried to put you off with excuses like, "I'm busy. Another time," the way your brother did. He had the patience to teach you to read words in Arabic, even if you didn't learn any of them, because Arabic letters are just as scared of you as the Hebrew ones. And don't ever forget that Mohammed gave you Johnny Weissmuller as a present when he was a week-old puppy, saying that a boy without parents had a heart overflowing with love and needed to give it to someone.

The second Uzik inside me was the real troublemaker. All the nasty names fit him. "Blockhead" and "brat", "rascal" and "smart-aleck", "*paskundyak*," "*shmendrik*" and "*momser*", "hooligan" and "wise guy" and "*Aza'ar*", in all the languages they spoke in our village. The last name, *Aza'ar*, in Arabic, was Mohammed's, but he only said it with love. I secretly enjoyed the name-calling. It made me something special in the village, not just some pathetic little orphan who'd become a burden on his Aunt Miriam's shoulders.

The other Uzik argued that the secret was dangerous. What would happen if Mohammed unintentionally told someone in his village that we were hiding guns. There are plenty of Arabs looking for revenge, and they might come in the middle of the night and settle the score with us. And I had to think about the British too, who were spying on us from the other side of the fence, and if, heaven forbid, one of them should find out, God help Imri and the fellows from the van.

That whole night, the soft words Mohammed whispered into his horse's ear kept running through my mind. What should I do? Who could I ask for advice? I tossed and turned in bed. Anna's a foreigner. And I mustn't forget for a minute that the Englishman, Charles Timothy Parker, called her "Annie" and promised her, "We shall meet again." And anyway, she wasn't my sister-in-law anymore. She was just a Polish woman staying with us until she found her relatives, and then we wouldn't hear from her anymore. And I wouldn't dare ask Imri, even if he were home.

What do you do if you have to be loyal to two people at the same time, Imri? I didn't want to choose. You had to, because that's what being grown-up meant, but I didn't want to. Both Uziks tortured me. I didn't even feel like playing Tarzan and sliding down from my window on my rope. That wouldn't make me feel better either.

I tried to talk to my mother in the air, and I even called to my father. But there was no answer. I had no idea how Aunt Miriam did that. In the morning, I whispered the secret into Johnny Weissmuller's ear, because what good is a secret if you can never tell it to anybody? But Johnny Weissmuller—a hairy creature who had no words, only barks—couldn't give me any advice either.

———

In the morning, Anna was writing letters.

She was sitting at the kitchen table, her hand racing across the paper, making line after line of beautiful round letters appear, like a magician. I was never jealous of people who knew how to read and write, but now, a kind of arrow passed through me and was gone in a flash. Maybe one of the Uziks that was running around inside me secretly wanted to be an excellent pupil like Zionka.

Anna wrote one letter after the other. I examined her from every angle. Her bent head, her hair gathered into a bun on her neck, and the special gesture she made unconsciously, pressing her fingers to the center of her forehead, as if collecting her thoughts, to keep them from escaping. Then I saw her face, lit by a strip of light. Every time I moved, I saw a different Anna. She was so immersed in her writing that she didn't notice me standing in front of her, blocking the light, on my way to school.

Who was she writing so much to? Since Imri had gone, she'd been spending hours over those pages, practically drowning in them, more than our teacher in school. How much more of an effort could I make to read and write? No matter how hard I tried, they told me it wasn't enough. Deep down, I was sorry I didn't know how to read. But only when I thought about what would happen if Zionka decided to send me a letter and I didn't understand it. And if I had something very important to tell Zionka and she was far away, how would I write to her? Maybe, by that time every house would have a magical device, and then no one would ever have to learn how to read and write, except the ones who really wanted to.

Every day, Anna waited for the mailman. She left the house and waited for him at the end of the street. And she looked disappointed when no letter arrived for her.

I watched her hand as it added line after line to the white paper until it was all black. Every time I tried to read, my head hurt, and I started hearing words that weren't written on the page. The letters were busy dancing their complicated dance, and I put my hand on them, tried to catch them, but couldn't. I thought it was strange that written words had so much power. That they could change your mood in an instant.

When Anna got a letter, her face glowed and she read it as she walked, gliding along the street to our house, completely unaware of what was going on around her. Once, Zusia the wagon driver almost ran her over, and it wasn't till he shouted a curse in Russian at her that she moved aside and kept on reading. I even saw her reading in the hen house, and she didn't even notice the chicks pecking away at the hem of her dress.

Anna said that when you read, everything comes alive, and I felt hopeless. I asked myself if I would ever be able to write a word to my mother in the air. Maybe then, I would feel that she's just in a far-off country, like Poland.

Anna didn't raise her head. I'd already discovered that she could write in the dark too, because she even wrote letters at night. She licked the envelopes and the letters piled up next to her. She probably had a bigger family than Mohammed.

I couldn't control myself any longer.

"Who are you writing to?" I asked her.

"To my mother and father, and my older brothers, who have their own families, and to my sisters-in-law and my girlfriends who are still in Poland, and to my little sister. She's exactly your age, only she's not a '*zhulik*' like you.

I clenched and unclenched my fists.

"Is that another nasty name?"

"It's Polish for 'mischievous'," Anna said. Not everything that sounds insulting is really meant that way. "'*Zhulik*' is said affectionately." I immediately thought of the name Mohammed called me, "*Aza'ar*," and I waited for her to ruffle my hair, the way he did when he called me that.

Uzik *Zhulik*—it even rhymed.

Something was bothering her. Something she'd wanted to ask for a long time, but hadn't dared.

"Why does your aunt always talk to herself?"

I burst out laughing. "She's not talking to herself. She's talking to dead people."

Anna was shocked. Right then and there, she had something to write to her family in Poland. Palestine really is a crazy country.

I wanted to reassure her.

"Don't be afraid, Anna, it isn't just any old dead people. It's my mother." But she didn't look reassured. Anna didn't know that my mother died on the day I was born, and I didn't plan to tell her.

I said, "If your little sister came here, she could be Zionka's friend."

"And yours too?"

My eyes avoided her gaze. I tightened my school bag on my back as if I were in a hurry.

"What do you write to her?"

Anna said that she wrote to her about life in Palestine, how different everything was here. The people reading those letters in Poland thought she had a vivid imagination.

No one wears a fur coat here, because it never snows. There are always leaves on the trees, because they don't fall off in autumn, and they're dusty, as if someone forgot to air them out in time. And she still hadn't seen a river like the one that flows near Lutsk. And the honey had a special taste that sticks to your tongue for a long time, and Anna also said that we eat with our hands and talk too loudly and push when we're waiting in line and our jokes are hard to understand.

And she wrote about Aunt Miriam too, and about Johnny Weissmuller and about ... "About me?"

For a minute, I was scared she might've discovered the guns.

Anna smiled, as if she were hiding a sweet secret, not a dangerous one, like mine.

"It's too bad you can't talk to your little sister with the magical device."

Anna said, "Telephone."

I'd already heard that word, but I'd forgotten it.

She said they had one on the desk in the English Consulate in Warsaw. It was black and had a dial that spun around and numbers. The English clerk had picked up the receiver. Anna and Imri had heard every word that was said on the other end.

"Who answered him from the other room?"

Anna said, "It was much further away. He talked to someone in Palestine."

I said, "If your little sister wants to immigrate to Palestine, she'll have to find a boy here who'll agree to marry her so she can get a certificate." I thought Anna would laugh, but a thin blanket seemed to suddenly cover her face.

"They don't want to come. They're angry at me for leaving. They think I made a terrible mistake and that one day, I'll pay a heavy price for it."

And I had been sure that all the Jews in the world were waiting in line to join us here.

Anna licked the last envelope and gently pressed down the triangle on the back. "They say this country has no future. Despite all the promises, the Jews will not have a country of their own."

Then I understood why they took their time answering her letters, and I felt a little sorry for her. Maybe when Anna writes, she feels the way I do when I try to talk to my mother in the air.

I said, "Tell them that we're fine here. You can even lie to them. You know, you can do that for the sake of the homeland."

Anna said a homeland is not sacred. I asked myself if she would dare say such a thing to Imri, but I'm not him. My teacher would also have been shocked to hear her. And then she said that she was worried about her loved ones who were there, in Poland. They didn't understand that a savage storm was brewing.

As she gathered up all the letters, one fell. It landed, like a white butterfly, under the table. I wanted to bend down, but Anna beat me to it. She knelt, and the bun of hair lying on her neck came undone. For a minute, I was taller than she was. Her whisper rose towards me. "A terrible disaster is going to happen there."

Mohammed

He will forget you twice a year. For a short while, you will no longer be his master, he will devote himself to another, a female master. Don't be jealous, Aza'ar, Allah has decreed it. This is the season that is conceived inside the body of the female, repeated in the spring and the fall, the way the sun goes down behind the olive trees and rises again tomorrow. The dog will pursue her throughout the entire land, will lie in wait for her, will crouch beside her lair day and night, until she responds to him. And you, his friend, whom he has loved since the dawn of his childhood, are as far from him now as if you had climbed up to the sky. With the special sense of smell that dogs have, the lucky one will find his mate, will follow her far beyond this river or that.

And only after his passion has been spent, and the season has passed, will he make his way back to you.

It isn't a final parting, Aza'ar. It is Allah's decree, so that our tongues may taste the onion of longing and torment before they taste the honey, for only then will we love even more that which has almost been taken from us.

Chapter 11

In school, my teacher asked me what we'd learned in our last lesson. Even without knowing how to read or write, I remembered better than the ones who wrote everything down in their notebook, and copied from the board, word for word.

I stood up tall, like Tarzan before he leaps. All eyes were on me. I could feel Zionka's gaze.

I spoke fluently, as if every boring textbook were flowing through me. I didn't know how they'd gotten inside me. My teacher's mouth hung open like a fish.

I felt like one of the leaders of the community giving a speech at a meeting in the village Committee House. My voice rose, and I waved my arms around enthusiastically.

"The Greeks won!" I shouted. "The battle with the Persians took place in a small town called Marathon. A messenger was sent to Athens. He ran forty-two kilometers without stopping, without drinking, without resting, only to tell the far-off Athenians about the victory, and after he'd told them, the runner fell down dead."

You could've heard a pin drop in the classroom. Something that had happened thousands of years ago had become real. And I thought it was a great idea for a movie. Johnny Weissmuller would lead the small Greek army and would drive the Persians back to their homeland, and then he would take on the job of informing the Greeks in Athens of the victory. He would run easily, not a drop of sweat running down his forehead, and after he'd told them about the victory, his muscles would cramp and he would roar his famous roar.

Everybody burst out laughing. Even my teacher smiled. I was surprised he'd also heard of Tarzan. I didn't think teachers went to the movies.

He said, "You see, children. The few against the many. The Persians may have had a big, strong army, but the Greeks had greater military skills, because they never stopped training, and you must remember, children, that the most important thing is the spirit of battle the Greeks had. They defended their homeland against a foreign conqueror."

The whole class cheered, as if they were at a soccer match. The teacher shushed them, "Athens was temporarily saved from destruction."

The room was again silent. It wasn't very nice to hear that victory could be temporary, and when Athens was destroyed, after many years and more battles, it never rose again. Maybe there was no one to tell them in advance about the catastrophe.

Zionka raised her hand and said that there was a new leader in Germany, Adolph Hitler, who they called "Fuehrer," and he was stirring up the mobs to shout "Jews, get out!" and threatening to kill them all. Zionka sounded worried, just like Anna.

The teacher dismissed what she said. "Others have oppressed the Jews before him. From Haman to

Chmielnicki. Nevertheless, they all disappeared from the face of the earth, and we still exist. There's no need to be frightened of speeches given by leaders. They want to be popular with the rabble. Hitler doesn't mean what he says. Those are just idle threats." The bell cut him off just as he was asking us to give other examples of tyrants.

During recess, Zionka said that if, God forbid, anything happened, we could warn each other through the tin cans on the string.

"Telephone," I said proudly. Zionka suspected I'd already spoken into the real thing without telling her.

The teacher wrote "Excellent" next to my name in his marking book and didn't threaten to keep me down any more. I wanted to be happy about my victory, to feel like the runner from Marathon, but something spoiled it. If he fell down and died, who did his children share their happiness with? Did they talk to the runner in the air without getting an answer?

———

After school, Johnny Weissmuller and I went to play soccer. Anna was walking up the street in the direction of the village post office. Johnny Weissmuller ran to her, matching his steps to hers. I saw a tall woman and a big brown dog walking away from me. I thought gloomily, how would I explain to Johnny Weissmuller that she'd be leaving soon? I'd have to consult with Mohammed, to ask him how to say goodbye.

I ran and caught up to them. Anna was waiting. I asked her for the bundle of letters and raised them to my nose. I explained to her how much I loved the smell of mail. For a long time, I hadn't wanted to collect stamps, because you couldn't organize them according to countries if you couldn't read, but Zionka convinced me that there was another way to arrange my album.

The stamps in my album were arranged according to color. I had a whole page of red ones and a page of yellow ones and half a page of orange ones and two rows of blue ones, and green was the only color I didn't have.

Because I didn't know how to read, it was hard for me to trade stamps, but even so, I thought my collection was more beautiful. Like a flowering field on the most spring-like day. Zionka warned me to hide the album from the bees.

I'd been hoping my collection would grow after Anna came. She promised to give me every stamp that arrived from Poland. I loved the post office, and I was willing to lick every stamp and seal every envelope they had. The taste of the glue was nothing like the taste of honey, but it stayed on your tongue for a long time, like honey did.

We met Aharonchik the baker, who was walking towards us. The newspaper, *The Truth*, which had come that day from Russia, was sticking out of his overall pocket. I knew that, for a whole month, we'd be hearing over and over again the news from the communist paradise, until the next issue arrived in the mail. Aharonchik never gave me stamps, because stamp collecting was a "bourgeois hobby," and anyway, soon the world wouldn't be divided into countries. Aharonchik said to Anna, "The communists will rule your country one day too," and that bothered her, because she didn't consider Poland "her country" anymore.

As we walked into the post office, I heard Ephraim

Perlmutter, the watchmaker, and his wife Mali whispering. "Imri doesn't know what to do with her. No one's managed to locate her relatives."

Ephraim Perlmutter shushed his wife, "Sssh," and pointed to Anna.

Johnny Weissmuller was barking outside. I had tied him to the door so he wouldn't run off to the English base. I didn't know whether Anna understood the gossip, because she still didn't know Hebrew. But I was sure she felt that they were talking about her. That happened to me too, even when people were talking in a different language.

Anna put the bundle of letters on the counter. Ezra Yacobi, the post office manager, added up the bill out loud and gave her the stamps.

I took one and licked it. Then I said, "Someday, people won't write letters anymore. They'll just talk on the telephone."

Anna said she wasn't so sure. There are people who can express in writing what they cannot say, and Ezra Yacobi bent down to me and promised that they would soon be putting a telephone in his post office, in addition to the one in the Committee House. I smiled at Ezra as if I had swallowed a whole jar of honey, and volunteered to help if only I could get to speak into his telephone one day.

"What can you write that you can't say?" I asked, puzzled.

Anna smiled. She also bent down to me and whispered in my ear, "I love you."

Ezra Yacobi listened in on our conversation. "Don't

ruin my business, you *momser*," he said, and laughed.

One of the letters was especially thick. I had to paste a long row of stamps on it.

"Who is this one for?"

Anna pushed the envelope in front of my face. "Try to read it."

I tried to avoid looking at it. My head was starting to hurt again. The post office was empty.

Anna said, "It's so easy. You just have to decide that you want to."

The letters were jumping around in front of me, glittering. Some of them pushed in front and I couldn't see where a word began and where it ended, and then the envelope was blinding me. I pushed it away from me. Johnny Weissmuller barked again outside.

Anna said, "I'm sending this letter to Imri."

I turned my back to her. I could still see the envelope glimmering. Ezra Yacobi opened the big sack of mail and I threw all the letters inside. I didn't want to tell Anna what I thought of letters traveling to far-off places. The words a person wrote were what he meant only at the time he wrote them. What happened if they stopped being right when they reached their destination? Someone who said "I love you" face to face was taking less of a risk. I was trembling a little, because that was the first time in my life someone said those words to me.

The letter to Imri was the last one to land, and it stayed on top of the pile. The sack looked heavy. Ezra Yacobi tied it with a string, mumbling and singing, "And make us reach our desired destination for life, gladness and peace." On Saturdays and holidays, he was the cantor in our synagogue.

Anna said, "That's the prayer offered before a journey. It protects you against danger. My father blessed Imri and me before we left." She whispered the word "father" so as not to hurt me, because I didn't have one.

On the way home, we saw some children playing soccer. They called to me to join the game, but I ignored them. In the Committee House, the choir was rehearsing for some celebration. "We've come to Eretz Israel to build and be built," they sang.

Anna didn't know the song.

I asked, "If you had to do something that would harm Eretz Israel or Poland ... what would you do if you had to be loyal to both homelands?"

Anna said, "That's easy. I've already made my choice."

I tried again. "And what do you do if you have to keep a secret from your best friend in the whole world?"

Anna listened attentively, but I didn't know if it was to me or to the choir.

"That's hard. Secrets hurt. They sting you inside."

I said, "A bee dies after it stings."

And Anna said, "Only the poison remains."

The choir repeated the same song, sounding like a broken record on the gramophone. I was sure that even Johnny Weissmuller could already bark out that song. "And make us reach our desired destination," those were the words that stuck in my mind. On the way home, I asked myself why there was no blessing for the ones who stay behind. They needed a blessing too and some encouragement to continue, and I was jealous of Anna for having parents.

Aunt Miriam

That day, you shook me by the shoulders, my sister. Don't give in, Miriam, you said, don't give up your man, but I, a good Jewish girl, didn't dare to go against my father's will. And my father sent the wagoner away just because he didn't come from a good family. If Zusia had at least fought for me, but he backed off without a word. Three months later, if you remember, they made a match for him with a woman from another village. Now, I look at him and find it hard to believe I ever wanted that man. He curses and beats his horse. He has nothing left of a suitor's charm. Maybe he really wasn't good enough. That's how you console me. I hear you very well, my sister. Only the rabbi believes me. He's a good man, a widower looking for a wife. I pour him hot tea in your beautiful china cups, he smiles pleasantly at me, and my cheeks suddenly burn. What do you think of that, my sister? Even if the match between Anna and Imri doesn't work out, I thank you for sending her to us. She is a glowing light in your house, my sister, walking through the rooms that once were yours, and the flesh, against its will, lives. Now, after such a long sleep, my body speaks to me, and I remember that I too am a woman. It was almost too late for me. Your older son is more like you every day.

I remember how father explained the wisdom of Maimonides. The male and female reproductive organs are similar, except that the male organs are external and the female, internal. That is why opposites attract. Even if I had wanted to, I couldn't have stopped what was going on between them. It was never like that with me. Zusia asked for my hand and I agreed, in the usual way. I don't remember any passion or desire.

Chapter 12

Weeks passed, and it was as if Imri had disappeared. We didn't get any letters or regards from him. Aunt Miriam was so worried that she sent Zusia the wagoner to Tel Aviv to look for the boys from the van. Zusia even went to the Jewish Agency offices and pestered some distant cousin of his who worked in the settlement department, and the cousin told him to calm down, everything was fine. Even though Zusia told Aunt Miriam, "You know Imri, he'll manage in any situation," she was very frightened. Just let him not do anything foolish and be tempted to go to Germany. That Hitler, that monster, may his name and memory be cursed, and those Nazis with their swastikas who scream "Jews, get out!" gave her nightmares.

To calm her down, I quoted my teacher, "Those are idle threats," but even I wasn't convinced.

Anna was sad. I didn't know whether Imri had promised her anything, but if he had, he seemed to have forgotten it. I tried to cheer her up, to joke, "You see, why should anybody write letters? That thick letter probably got lost on the way," but I didn't think that made her feel better. I waited for a chance to return the stolen candlestick to her trunk. Every day, I said to myself, tonight I'll undo that miserable prank of mine, but I still didn't have the courage to sneak into her room again and see those wet stripes on her cheeks. There were some pictures I'd rather not see.

On Friday nights, Anna lit one candle. Aunt Miriam was sure it was a Polish custom. She gave my mother in the air a long, complicated explanation about the fact that when a person is alone, without his family, he lights only one candle in the hope that someday, the pair would be reunited. Anna covered her face with her hands. Her lips moved in prayer and her straight back shook slightly.

Finally, I swore I would return the candlestick to Anna when I could add a a small piece of paper on which I'd written "I'm sorry." I was practicing, I really was trying, but the letters all joined together into a single black line and you couldn't read them. I was too embarrassed to ask Zionka to help me. In the meantime, only in the meantime, the candlestick was under my bed, a companion for Tarzan's rope.

Winter was on its way. It got colder. The bees stayed in their hives and the harvesting season ended. I locked the toolshed and, in front of the door, I built a doghouse for Johnny Weissmuller, so he could keep an eye on who went in and who came out. I tried to teach him to bark the famous Tarzan roar, but he didn't learn. His tail drooped and he looked the way I did when they tried to make me learn to read and write.

Before I put the hives and the honeycombs inside the shed, I moved Grandfather's old clay pots and pulled open the small door. The guns were there. I took one out. It was a Radom, a nine-millimeter pistol made in Poland. I recognized it right away, because the kids in my class loved guns and liked to rank them, which of them was more efficient and which was more deadly, and Herzl Fleischer even bragged that he could hit the bull's-eye like a grown-up.

He called himself a "gun collector," but it was his father who bought guns from the last century and hung them on the wall. Napoleonic rifles, rifles from the time of Queen Maria Theresa of Austria, bullets from the time of Queen Victoria, and rifles from the time of the Prussian King, Wilhelm. He also had Turkish Mausers made in Germany, and Winchester and Enfield rifles with long barrels. During recess, Herzl Fleischer would tell Zionka about the first rifle in the family's collection, the one his grandfather had used to chase off three Arab attackers. Zionka listened. She really was the politest girl in the village, and she only commented a couple of times that it was better to collect stamps, but she stayed next to him anyway.

The pistol took up almost my whole hand. It had a black handle with a triangular symbol that had something written on it. It was the color of steel, an object the size of a toy that could kill someone instantly. Someone who had a mother and father, and maybe children, someone with people who loved him, and who loved other people. Even though my hand was wrapped around the gun, it didn't warm up from the contact with my fingers. At recess, Herzl Fleischer told Zionka that if we had had guns five and half years ago, during the riots, we could have defended ourselves.

I suddenly heard Johnny Weissmuller barking. My heart raced. I pushed the gun into the old beehive and slammed the small door shut, but I couldn't pull over grandfather's old clay pots to cover the hiding place. My hands shook. I could hardly control them.

I went outside and leaned against the door, blocking the entrance with my body.

Mohammed waved at me. Johnny was licking his hand.

"*Ahalan ve'sahalan, Aza'ar*. Did you say goodbye to the bees? Did you wish them a sweet winter?"

I nodded. I couldn't speak. The sting inside me was burning so much.

Mohammed said, "We'll meet again in the spring, with God's help. Come to the village to buy new queens. Where's your big brother's new wife? Is she talking yet?"

I nodded again, like a mute. Aunt Miriam warned me not to talk about Imri when Mohammed was around, and not to say anything about a fictitious marriage. Your goy doesn't have to know everything, she said.

I was furious. Aunt Miriam said, "If you read books, you would know." I don't want to feel like someone's after me, Aunt Miriam. Anna had whispered in my ear, "I love you," but she didn't mean me.

Mohammed touched my head. "Are you sick, *Aza'ar*? Maybe you should come for a visit to my village? We'll ride. The horse misses you."

"Missing someone" was an expression that Zionka's mother and Mali Perlmutter would use. That was something I didn't want to talk about. Sometimes, I felt I'd lost out by not knowing my mother and father, and

I was jealous of Imri, who had known them. Even if I did learn how to write someday, I would never put that expression on paper.

"How do you know the horse misses me, Mohammed?" There were times when I was suspicious too. Mohammed said, "Sometimes I whisper into his ear, and sometimes he whispers back to me. But nobody ever sees it. It's our secret."

The sting inside me was still burning, and I blocked the entrance to the toolshed. Mohammed wanted to help me organize the equipment for the winter, but I said no. He was a little surprised, but didn't say anything.

"Are you cold?" he asked, worried, and was already taking off his kaffiyeh so he could wrap me up in it. "What prank did you play today, my little *Aza'ar*? Did you hide Zionka's duck in the toolshed?"

I trembled, and slowly pulled the door of the shed until it slammed.

"There's a story about the leader of the village, the mukhtar," Mohammed said. "His horse knew how to speak, but opened his mouth only in the presence of his master. When there were other people around, the horse would whinny and neigh. Nobody believed the mukhtar had a talking horse. Behind his back, they lamented, our mukhtar is mad, he sees things. Allah be praised."

Johnny Weissmuller listened to the story too, crouched at Mohammed's feet, looking up at him with moist eyes. I thought Mohammed was the best person to make up new stories for the Johnny Weissmuller in the movies. You didn't have to know how to write. You just had to close your eyes and the pictures moved.

Mohammed kept on spinning his tale, and I was watching a movie.

"The mukhtar was furious. One day, when he was out riding his horse in the olive grove, he complained to his horse, 'Why do you humiliate me this way? Why don't you open your mouth and talk when other people are around?' The horse said, 'When people are convinced of something, they won't believe anything else, even if they see it with their own eyes. Even if I talk to them with words as sweet as honey, they will hear only whinnies and neighs'."

We heard Johnny Weissmuller gurgle with pleasure. He was fascinated. I suddenly saw a hand petting him. We didn't hear Anna's steps. We didn't know she'd come outside. She was close, snuggling my dog in her arms, watching the two of us, and she said, "I'm listening to the sounds of the language. I'm sure it's a lovely story."

Mohammed shook her hand and asked me to translate.

"It really happened," he explained to Anna, "and that isn't the end of the story. The mukhtar had a daughter, an innocent girl with eyes like gray velvet. She was the only one who believed her father. Although she had never heard the horse speak, and she had no proof that the mukhtar's claim was true, she felt that her father was not wrong."

Anna was enchanted. Later, she said that listening to Mohammed was like reading a book. She tried very hard to understand his language. For a minute, I thought she had succeeded in catching a word or two.

Mohammed said, and I translated, "You have acted wisely. It is good that you have come to Palestine. The child is ill. He should be taken care of. He is an orphan. You will be 'the mother of Uzik'."

Mohammed was the first person to praise Anna for her decision to come to Palestine. I thought that, in her heart of hearts, she thanked him, and maybe was encouraged. After that, she called me "Mukhtar."

Mohammed tied his kaffiyeh around my head. It was wide, and its ends reached the ground. The chills were gone. The sting inside me had been removed without my feeling it.

Mohammed was about to leave. I didn't believe for a minute that his story had really happened. I'm not a gullible young girl with gray velvet eyes who believes everything like a blind bee. If dead people don't answer when you ask them a question, and they were once people, how could a horse talk?

Anna had become sad too. Maybe because she hadn't believed her father and left her house against his wishes.

I ran after Mohammed. I wanted to return his kaffiyeh. He wouldn't take it. "In the spring, with God's help, when you come to visit my village," and he pointed to Anna too.

Chapter 13

"Tell me, rabbi, how many times is a person allowed to get married and divorced?"

"The Almighty, blessed be His name, didn't say. He left it up to each individual man and woman."

"And it's all right with Him, rabbi, for you to lie, even if it's only to the English and for the sake of the homeland? After all, it does say in the Torah 'Thou shalt not give false testimony'."

The teapot fell over. The boiling water spilled onto the Aunt Miriam's best tablecloth.

We were sitting in the living room. The rabbi was holding his weekly cup of tea, complimenting Aunt Miriam as if she had prepared a special drink. Aunt Miriam jumped up. She screamed as if a wasp were flying around inside her, and she didn't notice the stain that was spreading onto the carpet too.

"How dare you, you little smart-aleck? Is that a way to talk to a great biblical scholar? Your mother, may she rest in peace, should only forgive me. Her youngest child is driving me to distraction."

The rabbi tried to calm her down.

"Uziel is right. There is a point to his question. I will answer you, my boy. A rabbi is like any other person, and he will have to give an accounting of his deeds, like any other sinner."

A rabbi who sins?

I hoped my mother and father weren't being punished in heaven now. I'd like to postpone my own day of judgment, because, seeing a list of pranks like mine, even the Almighty, blessed be His name, might collapse.

I had another urgent question to ask the rabbi. Like Aharonchik the baker, the rabbi said that all people are equal, although I wasn't sure they were both talking about the same people and the same equality.

"Tell me, rabbi, if all people are equal, does that make God a communist?"

It was a good thing Aunt Miriam had left the room and didn't hear the question. The rabbi smiled, though. He said it wasn't important what you called Him, God was still God.

I looked at the rabbi as he spoke. He had a long beard and curled side locks. He wore a velvet hat over his black skullcap, and the wrinkles on his forehead got deeper every day. My thoughts wandered. I could see people I knew, but they were so different. They had nothing in common. The rabbi and me, for example. Imagine him sitting with his legs folded under him, listening to Mohammed's fairy tales about mukhtars and talking horses. Ridiculous. Or maybe getting down on his knees and proposing marriage to Aunt Miriam, an idea so far-fetched that I laughed to myself. And there were other strange pictures in my mind. Zionka's mother dancing a tango with Meir, the charming butcher, and Aharonchik singing the "Internationale" without anyone interrupting him, and Anna humming Arabic music that Fahtma, Mohammed's sister, taught her. And the English pilot, who I couldn't connect to anything except to Aunt Miriam and five o'clock tea, which meant that if you try hard enough, you can find some kind of connection between people who are complete opposites. Take Johnny Weissmuller, in the movies. I liked him a lot more than Tarzan, who was an English lord, but there was no way I could break the connection between the two. And sometimes thoughts passed through my mind that I could never tell anyone, especially not Aunt Miriam or the rabbi. Maybe God, may His name be blessed, is also "fictitious," and we just don't know it?

Anna was out taking a walk. She usually left the house when the rabbi came for his weekly visit. I sometimes thought he reminded her of something she would rather forget. Lately, she would wrap herself in the old coat Aunt Miriam took out of my mother's closet, and go out of the house. She'd buried the fur coat from Poland at the bottom of her trunk. She walked in the fields and apple orchards, examined the silk worms on the mulberry trees, and picked tangerines in Alter's groves. She once came back full of mosquito bites, and another time, she was all scratched up by thorns, but nothing could make her give up those walks. Yesterday, she came home dripping wet, saying she'd tried to drink the raindrops to see whether the rain here tasted different than it did in Lutsk. Aunt Miriam gave her a funny look and handed her Imri's towel. Anna walked all the way to the gate of the English air force base. I saw the silhouette of a man on a horse, watching her from the other side, but I couldn't tell who it was. She sometimes went up to the barbed wire, and they would speak quietly.

Anna saw our countryside with the eyes of a foreigner, so I suddenly saw it differently too, noticing details that had escaped me. The way the sky changed in winter and the clouds gathered like bees in a hive, and the color of Zionka's eyes when her mother was mad at her.

I was born here, like Mohammed, like Imri, so everything seemed natural to me. But if I'd suddenly landed in Poland, I would probably check out all the things that seemed natural to the Poles, and I would definitely get excited about a forest I'd never seen before, or about animals—like foxes and squirrels and wolves— that I'd only seen in pictures, and I would get especially enthusiastic about snow, because that's the only place where silent, white flakes drift down from the sky.

The rabbi said that God forgives even the worst sinners, because He is merciful and forgiving, and even the most virtuous of men could never reach the high position reformed sinners had, and I thought that I didn't want to reform, because I didn't want to give up the pranks I might sometime want to play in the future.

Aunt Miriam changed the tablecloth, apologized to the rabbi over and over again for the suffering I was causing him, and after she had put the kettle on again, Zionka suddenly burst into the room without knocking. She was all excited. I was sure the ducks had run off to the English air force base after Johnny Weissmuller.

"Imri's on his way!" Zionka cried, "He got married again!"

We rushed outside. The rabbi pressed his skullcap

onto his head so it wouldn't fly off in the wind, and Aunt Miriam ran out after him, mumbling, "Thank God, may His name be blessed," and "That we have lived to see this moment," and Zionka's mother also showed up, as usual.

They ran to the center of the village and I ran in the opposite direction. I had to tell Anna. Maybe some new Polish girl was standing near the post office or the committee house, introducing herself to Aharonchik the baker, waving around Imri's passport that had her name in it as his legal wife. What would happen if they met each other? The new one would say, "I'm Imri's present wife," and Anna would have to admit that she was his previous wife. And there were still two more weddings for the homeland on the way.

Everyone was gathered around Imri, hugging him, bombarding him with questions: who did he meet, and what was the situation in Europe, and was Hitler still threatening.

Imri listened patiently, but his eyes wandered over everybody's head. Anna was nowhere to be seen. Neither was the new wife.

Aunt Miriam began sobbing, "We were so worried. Weeks without a word. And you've gotten thinner, Imri, what will your mother say?" As if so many weddings and divorces didn't leave Imri time to eat.

Imri was loaded with packages. I picked up father's old valise, which was very heavy, and I tried to be funny, "Maybe you're dragging around all the Jews from Poland," but no one laughed.

At the center of the village, in the square in front of the post office, Imri opened his backpack and started giving out presents: he wrapped Aunt Miriam's head in a silk kerchief; he gave Zionka's mother a lace embroidered tablecloth; he gave Zionka a little doll dressed in the Polish national costume; for Aharonchik, he'd brought a packet of tobacco with a Soviet stamp on it; he gave Zusia a lucky horseshoe; and he didn't forget the rabbi either. He gave him a prayer book from the seventeenth century that he had gotten in the rabbinical school in a small town on the Czech border, after he promised the people of the town that he would add it to the holy books in a synagogue in Eretz Israel. The rabbi kissed the prayer book and said to Imri, "And you have come to redeem Zion."

I was the last one. Imri pulled a fishing rod out of his bag, saying, "And this is for my little brother, the only brother I have. The only one I will ever have."

"Brother"—such a simple, exact word. Nothing could be added to it, and nothing could be taken away from it. I loved him so much, and I never told him.

I had no idea where to go fishing, because there was no river near our village. We only had a water well and an irrigation ditch in Alter's citrus groves. Maybe someday, when Imri and I went to Tel Aviv to see Johnny Weissmuller in the movies again, we could go down to the sea and try to fish together.

Amid all the noise and excitement, Imri's eyes looked hard at me, and I read the question in them, "Where's Anna?" I was shocked, because I understood without letters and without words.

The small procession moved towards our house, and I insisted on carrying the heavy valise. Imri stopped and lit a Players, and in the meantime, Johnny Weissmuller arrived and jumped on Imri, licking him all over. It was now clear that Anna was close by.

She was standing at the door of the house, wrapped in my mother's old coat that Aunt Miriam had taken out of the closet for her. Imri stopped for a minute. Then he slowly walked towards her. She too hesitated. I saw a tall, slender woman swaying like a tree in a light breeze, and then she took a step towards him. They did not touch, only the distance between them became smaller.

I didn't want to call Imri's new wife my "sister-in-law," not even for a little while. And I didn't want to know what I should call Anna now. What was she to me? There were so few people who were something to me.

Johnny Weissmuller, who I can say with confidence is "my dog," was standing between them. I didn't hear what they said, if they talked at all. They still hadn't touched.

What were they to each other? I asked.

If a man and a woman married under a real wedding canopy, and the groom covered the bride's face with a real veil and gave her real wine to drink and broke a real glass—and it was still all fictitious—then was God, may His name be blessed, who is the most honest and just of all, taking part in the lie, or was He sitting up there in heaven and suffering?

I hadn't had time to tell the rabbi something I'd very much wanted to say to him. I couldn't take a chance that Aunt Miriam would have another outburst. My mother and father got married once and never got divorced for the sake of any homeland. They just died.

The Rabbi

And they shall be told, "Be fruitful and multiply and fill the land." That is the wish of the Creator. You are a woman, Miriam, and although I am a rabbi, I am also a man. Listen, Miriam, that is the way souls and bodies unite. When a child is created, the Almighty asks the angel in charge of the pregnancy to come to Him and He says: At this moment, a person is being conceived from someone's seed. Here is the drop, take it into your hand, protect it from harm, and plant the seed in the womb.

It is the Almighty, blessed be His name, who decrees what the fate of that drop will be. The entire history of a person is in the hand of the angel. But the Almighty, blessed be His name, does not decide whether a person will be righteous or evil. That is up to the person alone.

Chapter 14

The second bride's name was Tonya Greenbaum, and everyone called her Tonka.

None of us had ever seen her, except for Imri, of course, who had to.

But even so, all of us knew almost everything about her, much more than we knew about Anna. Zusia the wagoner had a cousin whose niece on his grandfather's side had a neighbor, who was also Polish, and she knew Tonka's family personally. Zusia told the whole village that Tonka was a modest and proper young lady from a good family, seven generations of rabbis, and she played the piano and spoke three languages, was an only child who would inherit everything from her father, and if any trouble came along, she had an uncle who moved to America after the First World War, and owned a textile factory on Seventh Avenue in New York. An excellent match. Everyone in the village said that if Imri had a brain in his head, he should keep on being Tonya Greenbaum's husband forever.

Zusia did not forget to emphasize the most important detail. Tonka was beautiful. She had many suitors, but didn't want any of them because she didn't think they were good enough. Our Imri had won the hand of this

Jewish princess from Vilnius, and he really should lose no time in going to the Jewish Agency to ask to be released from his obligation to marry two more times for the sake of the homeland, because if he stayed married to Tonka Greenbaum, he would have a great future ahead of him. Zusia was sure that the Jewish Agency people were sensitive and would understand Imri's feelings and, if it were necessary, Zusia was prepared to talk to his cousin on his mother's side, who worked in the Settlement Department, and ask her to pull some strings, because he was ready to do anything for Imri's happiness and, of course, for Aunt Miriam's, whose whole life had been one of suffering. I sometimes suspected that Zusia the wagoner was ready to do anything especially for Aunt Miriam. Zionka told me secretly that many years ago, he'd wanted to marry her. Aunt Miriam rejected him at the last minute, and no one knew why.

The gossip about Imri's second wife spread throughout the village, as if everyone had known her from the day she was born. Aharonchik described her in great detail to every customer who came in to buy half a bread or a braided challah for the Sabbath. Hair as golden as wheat on a collective farm, and deep blue eyes. A perfect figure and impeccable manners. An elegant and graceful woman, who wore only the latest Paris fashions, as if she had just stepped out of a magazine. A princess like her, the experts claimed, had yet to immigrate to Eretz Israel because she had suddenly become enamored of Zionism. It was obvious that she had fallen head over heels in love with our Imri. He had been granted a gift from heaven. Imri was set for life. All of us were, and

Aunt Miriam's troubles were over.

Zusia the wagoner was in high spirits. Tonka would soon arrive and the most beautiful new immigrant in Palestine would be living in our village. In the meantime, she was staying at the Bristol Garden guest house in Jerusalem, and Zusia explained to everyone that she was waiting until her enemy, Anna, went away.

Anna ignored it all, kept to her daily routine as if nothing had happened. She agreed to work in the hen house as usual and spent even more time with the chickens than she always did, probably because they didn't gossip like people.

I was curious to know what kind of present Imri had brought for Anna. I didn't notice that she had anything new, except for an old pair of khaki pants Aunt Miriam gave her. And maybe the Torah doesn't allow men to give presents to their divorced wives, so they can each start their new lives without any reminders of the past. They probably just erased Anna's name from Imri's passport and that was that.

Later, I found out that Imri had brought her letters from Lutsk. He went especially to her parents' house and came back with a bundle of letters tied with a string. Anna read, and tears flooded her cheeks. She learned that the letters she sent from Ezra Yacobi's post office had never reached their destination. Her mother's letters were also damp with tears. They had thought Anna was lost somewhere at the end of the earth, and they were even angrier at her for being carried away into such a mad escapade.

Even I had started to think she had made a mistake.

What would she do here alone? Relatives in Tel Aviv that she had never seen couldn't be considered family, and what kind of life would she have without a father and mother? At least I had Aunt Miriam, and I had Mohammed and a dog.

They sat on the porch. I was looking for Johnny Weissmuller, who had disappeared as usual. The bones I'd left him at lunchtime were still untouched in his bowl.

Anna was darning socks, taking them from a large wicker basket standing in front of her, near a ceramic pitcher filled with water. Imri's socks were in the basket too, and she patiently darned the holes in them. Aunt Miriam said, "That's enough, Anna. You'll ruin your eyes."

Anna replied, "I must finish."

I whistled for Johnny Weissmuller, and I even climbed onto Zionka's fence to look for the ducks, because lately, he had developed a special relationship with the Zionist duck.

Aunt Miriam said, "We've grown used to you, Anna, haven't we, troublemaker? Who will I talk to?"

Recently, she'd stopped bothering my mother and reporting every little thing to her, like how I was doing with my reading, although maybe Aunt Miriam had decided to keep quiet so as not to worry my mother about Imri's trips back and forth to Europe.

"We made a mistake," Anna said, and I didn't know whether she meant the marriage or the divorce.

I thought Imri was at his wit's end too. He got up and paced nervously around the porch. We heard the thunder of a far-off explosion. I thought they were shooting at the English base, and Imri said, "They never stop training, even at night." A picture of the Radom pistols flashed through my mind, and I couldn't decide whether to tell Imri that I'd discovered the hidden guns.

Aunt Miriam said to Imri, "Anna is a part of our household, " and she told him how the chickens clucked with joy when Anna arrived in the morning and didn't peck at her in anger when she gathered the eggs, and how devotedly she had tended to the bees through all the months of autumn, and how, since Anna had come to us, even I had calmed down, and my teacher said that I was improving and there were signs that I might start reading soon.

Imri said, "You're here, Anna, and that's what's important. I'll find a way, I promise." And I didn't understand what was bothering them. After all, it was already very clear how easy it was to get married and divorced.

Anna did not raise her head, and her precise movements hid her embarrassment. Between stitches, she sipped water from the ceramic pitcher. The hole in Imri's sock was especially large. I didn't think there was any point in darning it. It would be better to throw it away. Even Aunt Miriam was convinced that pair of socks was a lost cause. My Aunt was not generous with compliments. I didn't remember her ever being as gentle to anyone else as she was with Anna that night. Maybe it was something in the air. Imri's hand moved towards Anna and then stopped. At exactly that moment, her fingers were trying to thread a needle, without success.

I waited for Anna to say that she had to go back to

Poland. After that bundle of letters she got, Anna was even more worried about her parents and her little sister. I was working on a prank that would sneak them into the English quota for new immigrants. I had to see "Tarzan" again, so I could steal a good idea from it.

Imri muttered, "What a mess." They didn't tell me what they were so worried about. They didn't even care that Johnny Weissmuller had disappeared, and it was late already, even for a snoopy dog like him. I was so mad that I chewed him out in my mind: "You irresponsible show-off," "You miserable beast," and "You devil," but then I was sorry.

"So get divorced already!" I yelled at Imri. All we needed was for Tonka Greenbaum to suddenly show up here, that famous beauty whose name was stuck in his passport.

Imri gently took the needle and thread from Anna's hands and tried to thread it for her. He looked so helpless and ridiculous. I tried to imagine him drawing a Radom and aiming it at a target, the way Herzl Fleischer's father did, and I started laughing.

"Tonya Greenbaum refuses to give me a divorce," Imri said to me, and dropped the sock with the big hole onto the floor. Then he cried out, because he'd stuck himself with the needle.

Chapter 15

Whistling was no use. I had to give a full-throated roar for Johnny Weissmuller. Anna and Imri smiled and Aunt Miriam moaned, "The situation's getting worse from day to day".

I was beginning to worry about the dog. He had never come home so late before. Maybe he had been kidnapped by a tribe of cruel pygmies who were about to toss him into a pit where at this very moment a huge gorilla was opening its big black maw. That scene in the movie was so scary that I kept my eyes closed all through it.

Imri licked the finger he had pricked with Anna's needle.

"How does your own blood taste?" I asked.

"You're movie-struck," Imri smiled. "Too bad I took you to Tel Aviv, Uzik. Tarzan doesn't really exist."

"But Johnny Weissmuller does!" I protested. "Swimming champion of the world. You saw for yourself how he crossed that dangerous river with those crocodiles breathing down his neck."

Nothing ever runs off the movie screen. The pictures are clear, they don't hurt my eyes and I feel as if I'm right up there, part of them. When I asked Anna whether she had seen the movie, she replied that she had read the book about Tarzan.

"A book is not the same thing as a movie," I told her, and I wanted to promise her that one day I would take her to the Beit Ha'am Cinema in Tel Aviv, but I kept quiet. Maybe Imri wanted to invite her, although now he couldn't go out with anyone but his second wife.

The flame of the kerosene lamp drove away the mosquitoes. I was suddenly filled with a sense of well-being. They weren't a married couple, but they were together in some other way. I stopped worrying about Johnny Weissmuller. Dogs always come home, that's what Mohammed says. Aunt Miriam went inside to make tea for us. She had baked a cake to celebrate Imri's return, and the delicious smell drifted outside from the kitchen. Imri breathed deeply and said it was the smell of home. I thought he was exaggerating—the smell of cake is nothing more than the smell of cake.

There was a kind of peacefulness on the porch. Even Zionka's ducks had stopped quacking. Poland was far away now, and Palestine seemed to be the safest place in the world. I thought that we could easily get rid of Tonka Greenbaum, Imri's second wife. We just had to cross out her name on the passport, and that would be that. You didn't have to know how to read and write to draw a line. I wanted to tell them that, but I kept quiet, because Anna was busy rolling pairs of socks and putting them into the wicker basket. Imri pocketed the sock with the hole in it and got up to help her carry the basket inside. His hand brushed against her as if by accident.

We didn't hear any steps because the crickets had gotten carried away with the sound of their own voices.

111

The flame flickered, but not because of the wind. I saw him as if he had stepped out of a movie, half in light and half in shadow. My heart began to race, pounding like a horse's hooves.

Major Charles Timothy Parker stood in our yard right beside the tool shed. I almost yelled. An English pilot at our house? We were caught. All was lost. The thoughts were exploding in my mind. The Englishman's hands rose. I knew he had to be holding a rifle, and I whispered, "They're not guilty. I'm the one." But no one was listening. He stepped into the light. In his arms lay a quivering, furry body, whimpering faintly.

"I've brought the dog. He's injured. He crossed the fence into the base and the sentry shot him."

"Johnny!" The cry rose from within me, but no sound emerged. Deep inside me everything froze, the way it had that day my father's heart stopped beating. The leaves had been still then, the bees weren't flying, and I'd felt nothing.

I remember that I spoke to him. He was still alive, quivering. I didn't know if he could hear me. Zusia the wagoner and Zionka's mother pushed me away from him. Zionka wasn't there. I don't remember her being anywhere. After that day, I swore I would never, ever speak to the dead.

The English pilot looked me straight in the eye and said, "He's still alive!" We laid him down on the table between the ceramic pitcher and Anna's sewing box. Johnny Weissmuller was breathing heavily, his chest rising and falling. Every so often, his body jerked strangely.

I said to the dog, "I'll be your Tarzan, you'll see."

Aunt Miriam hurried inside and brought back some sheets. The Englishman rolled up his sleeves, the symbols of his rank disappearing, and announced that we had to remove the bullet. The vet who treated the animals in our village lived in a kibbutz five kilometers away, but if we went there, it might be too late. We couldn't go to get Mohammed either, because it wasn't safe to wander around at night near his village.

Imri burst into the toolshed, leaving the door wide open. He kicked grandfather's old clay pots aside, I heard them shattering, and he began grabbing up whatever he came across, knives, scissors, a basin, until he found the pliers we used to separate the slabs of beeswax from the hives.

"Hold him tight!" said Major Charles Timothy Parker.

Imri and Anna stood on either side of Johnny Weissmuller. I wanted to hold him too. He was my dog. Mine, *mine*. Aunt Miriam pulled me aside. "This is not for children," she said, trying to cover my eyes.

I told her that after what I saw the day my father died, I could see anything.

The wound was ugly. Scarier than the one on Tarzan's forehead. Johnny Weissmuller's red blood was pouring out of him, and I covered the hole with my hand to stop the flow. My father had not bled even one drop.

Imri hung the kerosene lamp on the hook over the toolshed door. You could see everything inside. Pictures of the old beehives and the rows of pistols passed through my mind like the frames of a movie running backwards.

Anna poured alcohol on the torn sheet to sterilize it. The Englishman said, "Now." He inserted the pliers. I closed my eyes and when I opened them, the bullet had been removed. A shriek burst forth from Johnny Weissmuller's throat, and maybe from my own. Something was tearing me apart inside.

"Please don't look, Uzik," Aunt Miriam said, and because her voice was so different, so imploring, I shifted my gaze to Anna. What I saw astonished me.

I thought she would've fainted or screamed at the sight of blood, but Anna was working deftly, holding Johnny Weissmuller firmly by the legs, following the Englishman's instructions to the letter, dipping sheets in water, cleansing the wound again and again.

How lucky that you're Anna and not Tonka Greenbaum.

Anna bandaged the wound, winding the strips of material around Johnny Weissmuller's body. She had a talent for doctoring. Major Charles Timothy Parker examined the bullet under the light. I have no idea what kind of bullet it was or why that was even important. He threw it as far as he could, past the castor tree. We heard the metal hit something, maybe the side of the toolshed. Had the Englishman seen what was inside?

He bent over my dog, petted his heaving back. "You'll live to play in a great many more movies, Johnny Weissmuller."

Major Parker took a deep breath. My dog was wrapped in white and his trembling was subsiding. His quivering body lay between Anna and the Englishman.

"Is this your husband?"

Anna nodded. She was getting to be a better liar. Maybe she was learning from the rabbi.

Imri extended his hand over Johnny Weissmuller's body.

The Englishman raised his own hands helplessly. They were covered with blood. His beautiful, pressed uniform was stained too, and the brass buttons were no longer shiny.

Imri put his hand back into his pocket and they didn't shake hands after all.

Major Parker asked, "You've returned?"

Imri nodded.

The Englishman said, "Women should not be left alone. Someone might suddenly appear and steal their hearts."

Aunt Miriam filled the basin with water and pushed it toward him. The Englishman immersed his hands, washing them again and again. The water turned red. Then she handed him a towel and he dried them slowly and thoroughly. You could tell right away that he was a commander who never lost control.

Aunt Miriam asked in Yiddish if he wanted a cup of tea. The Major understood the word "tea," and we could see him hesitating. I remembered that he missed the daily ritual, the delicate china cups and civilized conversation about the weather. And the way he looked at Anna ... I prayed he wouldn't call her "Annie." Finally, the Englishman politely declined the offer. He had to return to base, he explained, he was scheduled for a night flight.

Aunt Miriam didn't insist. She removed the basin and I hugged Johnny Weissmuller, asking him to please stay alive. I didn't blame him. Dead people aren't to blame for dying. I know that my father didn't choose to die. Maybe even Aunt Miriam would understand that some day. She spilled out the water behind the toolshed. Imri doused the lamp and locked the door of the shed. We stood in the darkness. The Englishman had been swallowed up by the trees and I listened to the blood and water being absorbed into the earth.

Chapter 16

I whispered soft words into his ear all night. I had to find new words, because Mohammed's were not enough. I described the whole movie from the minute the curtain opened like a giant veil hiding Africa behind it, waiting patiently for us to enter. I described picture after picture, and when I'd finished with the real movie, I made up a new one. Johnny Weissmuller did the impossible. In my movie, he did amazing things that left the audience with their mouths open. He carried Anna's mother and father and her little sister on his broad shoulders, and the English fell on their knees begging for mercy. In the last picture, they took off in their Hawkers and left our homeland. I whispered to my dog that he was stronger than the Johnny Weissmuller in movies. I was willing to lie. Not for the sake of the homeland, Johnny, but for an even more noble purpose. Because I couldn't lose someone I loved for the third time. No one, even the Almighty, may His name be blessed, will steal your heart from me. If that's called love, then I love you, Johnny Weissmuller.

The window was open. A cold wind blew inside. Johnny Weissmuller was trembling, and I wrapped him in my blanket. An airplane was circling in the sky above the village water tower, making sharp turns. I wanted to know what our country looked like to a hawk. Was it different at night than during the day? Maybe the Hawker could land on the banks of the river near Lutsk and pick up Anna's family, and tomorrow morning, when we woke up, they would be here.

I'm hugging you very, very tight, Johnny. Your mother also died giving birth. Do you remember how I fed you with an eyedropper every two hours? Mohammed told me how to drop the milk into your little mouth. You still hadn't opened your eyes. And I thought you were afraid to find out you had no mother, so I explained to you that now, I was your whole family. On the sixth day, I started feeding you with a bottle that had a rubber nipple, and when you were three weeks old, you started to walk, Johnny. Even then, you slept in my bed, because Mohammed said that the warmth of my body would keep you alive. Do you remember how Aunt Miriam carried on? She screamed, "Dogs and children do not sleep together."

The snowy crystal ball glowed in the dark. I hated it more every day. Nothing moved inside it, except for the snow, and only the wolf reminded me of Johnny Weissmuller, who was breathing heavily at my side, and I immediately pushed the thought out of my mind, because he was absolutely not allowed to be in such a cold place, or his roar would freeze.

I ask you, Johnny, how did the Englishman know where we lived? I'm not mad at you for showing him the way. I know you didn't mean for anything bad to happen to us. You only wanted to come home. I don't know what he saw in the toolshed, and even if he did see something, he did all he could to save you.

I dozed off beside him, still wearing my clothes stained with his blood, and the frozen silence kept waking me up. I checked his breathing, the way the elephant did when he was taking care of Tarzan, who was injured, shaking him with its trunk so he would wake up. I cannot bark into the air, Johnny. Please stay alive!

Imri and Anna were walking around downstairs. They were awake. I swear I'll return the stolen candlestick by the weekend, Anna, so you can finally light two candles for the Sabbath. I want Imri to watch you say the blessing over both of them.

Johnny Weissmuller was lying against me. When Mohammed had brought him to me—a two-day-old puppy—he said that from then on, I would be responsible for him. Responsibility is not a word for animals, Mohammed said. It was meant for people only. In the movie I made up, Tarzan even learned to cry, but not from me. The pictures got all mixed together in my mind, climbing over each other like the letters on the blackboard, and I couldn't tell the difference between what happened in the movies and what really happened.

I opened my eyes to a room flooded with light. Mohammed was at my side, gently removing the bandage from Johnny Weissmuller's body. At sunrise, Imri had driven Alter's van to get Mohammed. I breathed a sigh of relief. Everything would be all right now. Mohammed knew what to do.

He rubbed a special salve that Fahtma had made from plants on Johnny's wound. Anna bandaged him again, careful not to hurt him.

"We'll have to wait," Mohammed said. "He'll have to fight. You'll help him, Aza'ar. Someday, we'll take our revenge on the English."

Anna wanted to know what he was saying, and I translated.

"What good is revenge?" she asked.

Mohammed gave her an embarrassed look. "If someone does something bad to you, you must do likewise to him, or else you will be thought weak."

"And then what happens, Mukhtar? We shoot them, and they shoot us, and then we shoot back, and when will it all end?"

Mohammed said, "Blood is the price of blood," but he didn't sound so sure anymore, as if the words were coming from someone else's mouth. "There are people in our village who preach … maybe where you come from …" He sounded defensive.

"Blood has a price," Anna interrupted him, tightening the bandage. Johnny Weissmuller whimpered weakly. And I added, "Mohammed, don't forget that the Englishman saved him."

Mohammed said that people's customs and ideas don't change easily. If the Jews had returned to Palestine a few at a time over two thousand years, maybe the Arabs could have gotten used to them, but the people living here were frightened because the Jews wanted to come back all at once, like a flood after a drought.

Anna tried hard to understand what he was saying. She already knew a few words in Arabic. "Change," for example.

"Spread the salve on him every day. The wound will heal. Only the scar will remain," Mohammed said, helping her tie the last knot.

I tried to rerun the movie in my head. There had been no sign on Johnny Weissmuller's forehead of the bullet Harry the hunter had shot at him. You could call it a "fictitious" wound. Imri said they painted it on with a paintbrush. When Mohammed said goodbye to Anna, he called her "Uzik's mother" again. He hadn't heard about Tonka Greenbaum, who was staying at the Bristol Garden guest house in Jerusalem.

I said I would go to school only after Anna promised to watch over the injured Johnny Weissmuller. I warned her, "Don't leave him for a minute. So no one will try to steal his heart."

Anna said, "You see too many movies."

"Too many, Anna? But I've only seen one."

When I left the house, I saw Aunt Miriam poking around in the toolshed. For a minute, I was scared, because she never before found a reason to go into a place that was strictly my father's, but she came out holding the old baby's bottle that used to be mine when I was little. Anna raised her head and smiled at me. The last sight I saw was both of them feeding the dog hot milk. In my mind, I called Anna "the mother of Johnny."

———

On the way to school, everyone stopped me to ask how the patient was. In our village, news got around fast. Somebody told somebody else, who told somebody else, who told somebody else, and five minutes later, everyone knew.

Aharonchik came out of the bakery, patted me on the back and announced to all his customers that Johnny Weissmuller was a Jewish hero. Anyone injured by an enemy's bullet for the sake of the homeland deserved special respect. I didn't want to throw cold water on Aharonchik's enthusiasm. Johnny hadn't meant to go out on a daring mission. He just liked to run around on the English parade grounds, where there was so much open land and you could see the horizon.

I was tired and confused and I didn't listen to the teacher. He was saying that in the Middle Ages, all the Jews in Venice were herded onto an island called Ghetto. He wrote the name on the board. I looked over at Zionka's notebook and saw letters that didn't look anything like the word "Ghetto."

People living in Palestine thought it was the only country in existence. They couldn't imagine any other place. No matter how hard I tried, I couldn't understand any other place, but that didn't mean other places didn't exist. Other places existed even though I couldn't see them, on the other side of the wire fence of my mind, maybe inside the closed crystal ball. And they had earth and sky and mothers and fathers and children, and someone like me, or almost like me, except that I didn't know him and he didn't know me. And I also thought there were places in the world I would never see, but if they were in the movies, I could feel as if I were really there.

My teacher repeated the word "ghetto" over and over again so we wouldn't forget it, even though I'd learned it the first time.

If we could see other places on the screen, then we'd have to believe they existed. They always teach me that Eretz Israel is the homeland—the most important, dearest place in the world. But somebody else's place is the most important place in the world for him. And the strangest thing of all, the thing that made it so complicated, was that for the Jews and the Arabs, it was exactly the same place, except that each of them thought they were talking about a different place.

My head drooped. From somewhere far away, my teacher was explaining that the Jews in the ghetto of Venice were forced to wear a sign on their clothes so they could immediately be identified everywhere. A yellow patch, my teacher said, and I saw Zionka's golden hair.

My head dropped onto my desk, which was covered with names carved into it. My teacher felt so sorry for me that he let me sleep through the lesson. Zionka told me that later on our telephone.

I saw yellow spots floating on water, and then I drifted off.

Mohammed

Go after him, Aza'ar, Allah gave him qualities that we do no have. Dogs see creatures from the spirit world that human beings cannot.

Raise your head, Aza'ar, a large dog and a small dog are crouching over you. They are the only dogs I know that do not need a mate. They are zodiac signs, and they are separated by the Milky Way. Their ears prick up when Allah orders it and their barks shine upon you from afar. They carry His words from one side of the heavens to the other. And the heavens are larger than we can ever imagine. When the dog curls up at your feet, before your eyes close, hug him again and thank him. He saw your mother and father and brought you their love.

Chapter 17

In the afternoon, the Englishman returned and stood in our yard, holding a sprig of flowers. He waited with the patience of a disciplined soldier, and didn't dare to knock on the door. Anna had gone to the post office again, with a bundle of answers to the letters Imri had brought from Poland.

Aunt Miriam grumbled, "What's he doing here?" and stayed in the kitchen. "My invitation to tea was for yesterday, not today," she said, and she didn't sound as if she was talking to the air.

I sneaked out the back door to the toolshed to make sure the door was locked. It was a great look-out point for a spy.

Zionka also came into the yard, drew back for a minute, until that splendid uniform had worked its magic on her. The brass buttons once again reflected the light. There was no sign of blood. It was a starched pilot's uniform that smelled pleasantly of laundry soap. The Zionist duck waddled after Zionka. Wherever she went, he was right behind her.

"Are you the Englishman who saved Johnny Weissmuller?" Zionka asked in English. She was the most outstanding pupil in the whole school. Some people said she even surpassed Imri.

"I came to see how he is."

Zionka said, "Mohammed and Anna are taking care of him."

"Mohammed? Is that her husband's name?"

Zionka laughed. "Of course not. Her husband's name is Imri."

The Englishman said, "I can't distinguish between you. Jews, Arabs, you all look the same to me. And what's that?"

He was pointing to the toolshed.

Puzzled, Zionka asked, "Don't you have toolsheds in England?"

"I thought the couple lived in that shack. They've only just married, haven't they?"

I prayed Zionka wouldn't say they'd already managed to get divorced. But she avoided the trap. My Zionka was very sly.

"They were engaged for a long time," she said. "They wrote letters to each other."

The English pilot looked ridiculous with the sprig of flowers in his hand, waving it around nervously. The flowers had started falling.

"Where is Annie now?"

Zionka also knew how to lie when necessary. Our village, so I was finding out, was full of excellent liars. The rabbi and me, for example. Zionka ignored the "Annie."

"They've gone away. Do you know what a honeymoon is?"

The Englishman remarked, "He travels a great deal.

What does he buy when he's abroad?"

Zionka said that Imri sold honey. Our product was well-known throughout Europe. How could the English not have heard of the first Hebrew honey after two thousand years?

Right then, I jumped out of my comfortable look-out point. What did he want from us? It was true that he saved a Hebrew dog, but that didn't give him any right to poke around in our life.

"Major Parker!" I called.

He smiled broadly under his well-trimmed moustache when he saw me. I had to admit that he was much more impressive than Imri. He was taller than Anna, and he had broad shoulders. He just didn't know what to do with his hands. Exactly like Imri.

"Oh, here's the little Zionist that's mad about the movies. You can call me Charlie."

I said formally, "Johnny Weissmuller would like to thank you, sir."

"You should tie him up, little Zionist, so that he doesn't wander round in dangerous places. Our sentry was sure he had rabies."

I said that I hated for animals to be tied up. An animal is not a prisoner.

Major Parker laughed, "People are tied up too, only you can't see the ropes." In the meantime, he was looking around. "It's lovely here. Such peace and quiet. Do you keep your games in that toolshed?"

I said I wasn't a little kid, and he answered that adults play games too. His king, George the Fifth, had a room full of electric trains in his castle in Windsor, and he had a huge collection of toy soldiers that he moved around a large map that covered the entire floor of the castle. I thought that in another minute, he would invite me to play with his king.

"Perhaps you have movies in your toolshed, little Zionist? They're already filming a new Tarzan movie in Hollywood."

Hollywood again. Where is it?

Major Parker was the strangest man I'd ever met. It was a good thing that I was cleverer than he was, maybe because of all the pranks I'd played in my life. I understood what was behind his questions. He was looking for the pistols.

"Will she be returning soon?"

I hoped Anna would stay at the post office for a while longer and not appear at exactly that minute and expose my lies and Zionka's. The Englishman said he hoped the flowers on the sprig wouldn't wither before Annie returned.

"I was out on an early flight," said Major Parker, "and while I was landing, I saw a swarm of bees on a bush. Do you know what they say about a branch that a swarm of bees has landed on?"

I shook my head.

"They say that such a branch can awaken love. Do you need a bit of love, little Zionist?"

"I don't need anything!"

Zionka got angry, "And his name isn't 'little Zionist'!"

"Yes, yes. You're a big Zionist. Someday, if you wish, I'll take you for a spin in my Hawker. It's called the Nimrod Hawker, after the biblical hunter. You'll be able to see your Palestine from above and discover for yourself how small it really is."

The Englishman waved the branch, as if he were making sharp turn. For some reason, he was excited. One of the flowers caught on a button of his uniform. I didn't know how he had chased away the swarm of wild bees so he could break off the branch without getting stung.

He didn't ask anything else about my dog. He only asked me to give the sprig of flowers to Annie, and he gave the flower that had caught on his button to Zionka, bowing to her. When he had gone, I threw the branch as far as I could behind the toolshed. I was good at that because of all the practice I had throwing my socks at the Jewish National Fund collection box on my door. Then I went to see where it had fallen. Something was glittering in the grass, hidden under the castor tree. It was the bullet Major Parker had taken out of Johnny Weissmuller the night before.

Zionka held the flower and smelled it every now and then. I yelled at her, just like her mother did, "Throw it away. It's an Englishman's flower," and Zionka got red with anger and held on to the flower. She said, "It grew in our field, not in England."

Zionka's mother

If my husband would at least dance with me once, Mali. That's not such an unreasonable request, is it. He comes home once a week, his fingers swollen and bleeding from crushing the gravel they use for paving roads. He falls onto the bed like a sack of sorghum, and even in his dreams, he doesn't ask me to dance. When my father first promised me to him, before we stood under the wedding canopy, I was proud as a peacock. After all, no woman wants to be a virgin all her life, like our neighbor, Miriam. If it had been Meir then, the charming butcher, my life would be a different story today. But Meir still hadn't immigrated to Eretz Israel. What a fool I was, more foolish than the ducks in the yard. I'm always quacking after my husband, and he puts me off with "I'm too tired." Am I such a stranger to him? More of a stranger than that woman who just got off the boat from Poland? Or is it just an excuse, Mali? He's impotent. Swear to me you'll never reveal this terrible secret to another soul. After all, you're my best friend in the village.

The Torah commands, "You shall not diminish her food, her clothing or her marital rights." I've already secretly been to the Rabbi for advice. He told me that my husband is like the donkey drivers who transport goods on donkeys and are obligated to fulfill their duty only once a week. If I could turn back time, the way you repair the broken clocks in your shop, I would change places with Anna. What an idiot she was to leave Europe. That's where refinement and elegance are, where you can go dancing with barons and earls. Why even Casimir the First, King of Poland, married Ester'ka, a Jewish girl. Last night, I dreamt I was at a great ball. One step, two steps and the music twirled us around. A broad-shouldered man in a splendid uniform bowed to me, held me by the waist and whispered sweet nothings in my ear. All of a sudden, a hand shook me, and when I opened my eyes, I saw Zionka standing beside me, asking, "Momma, who are you singing to in the middle of the night? You almost fell out of bed." And because of my daughter, my dream had vanished.

Why was I destined to live in this scorching, neglected land that has no fancy dress balls or orchestras or muslin and silk dresses or green lawns you can roll around on with your man. Here, everyone knows everyone else, tongues wag and there is nowhere you can escape to. I want a husband who dances the tango, not one who crushes gravel for roads. You can believe me, Mali Perlmutter, when I tell you that I didn't even have a proper wedding party. No bridal dance and no musicians.

We'll get a divorce and put an end to it! It's no disgrace. We'll do what Imri and his Polish bride did. They're the real pioneers. They've paved the way.

Chapter 18

"And what in the world is that imperialist doing in our village?" Aharonchik the baker asked suspiciously. "Be very careful, *tovarish*. We are building a model society of workers—a proletariat. Repeat the word so you won't ever forget it. You don't have to write it. Listen carefully, Mujik. There is no place in the socialist world revolution for Englishmen who drink whisky and not vodka. We are now witnessing the decline of the British Empire. Someday, the best of the Hebrew youth will take refuge in the shadow of big brother Joseph Vissarionovich Stalin …"

We were in Shmariyahu's grocery. When Aharonchik didn't have any customers, he stayed in his neighbor's store, enthralling him with speeches. Shmariyahu was the only person in the village that listened avidly to all the news arriving from Russia in the newspaper, *Truth*. Meir, the charming butcher, suggested the pair join a commune and poked fun at Aharonchik, saying he was a capitalist like everyone else.

I looked at the shelves that surrounded me. All the food we put in our mouths was spread out in front of me. A barrel of oil and a barrel of herrings. Boxes of sugar and dried dates and figs and apricots, sacks of flour and salt and rice and lentils and beans. A tin of dried coconut, tins of Syrian cracked olives and pickles, and watermelon and sunflower seeds.

Aharonchik was carried away with his speech, waving his arms around like one of our great leaders, and Shmariyahu was listening with his mouth open. Aharonchik's influence was turning him into a communist too. I hoped a customer would come and release me. I had only one big brother, and I didn't need any Stalin who lived so far away. I remembered Aharonchik's first of May speech about that great leader, a speech that went on for two hours, until the whole audience walked off. Only Shmariyahu had stayed sitting alone in the first row, applauding and yelling, "Workers of the world, unite!"

I could hardly get a word in edgewise while Aharonchik was giving his speech. I had only come to the grocery to buy dried figs for Anna and fresh yogurt, but he was interested in when Tonka Greenbaum would finally show up in our village. Maybe he would manage to turn a beautiful bourgeoise into a loyal Bolshevik. Aharonchik added that Anna had to leave the village immediately and go to her relatives, because a man with two women was a scandal, and we couldn't allow our village to get a bad reputation in the Hebrew community.

I protested, "He only did it for the sake of the homeland."

"What about love?" a voice squeaked behind me. I turned around and saw Zionka holding half a loaf of a fresh black bread she had taken from the bakery. The fresh smell filled the air and I started to feel hungry.

Zionka couldn't resist, and she munched a piece of bread as she spoke.

"What does love have to do with it? Who needs love?" I grumbled, looking at the bread.

Aharonchik preached to Zionka about the miracles of communism, predicting a great future in the egalitarian society to come, when it would not matter whether a person was a Jew or a woman, because only the bourgeoisie consider a woman to be a means of production. Zionka was slowly finishing off the bread, and I decided that I couldn't take any more chances and had to get rid of the guns as fast as possible. Maybe Major Charles Timothy Parker would decide to come to our house again and trick Zionka. Next time, he'd find an excuse to go into the toolshed and look around, and he'd tell her he was looking for a game from Palestine to bring to his childish king.

I had no one to talk to about it. Imri was gone that morning. I heard Aunt Miriam explaining to my mother in the air that Imri was going to Jerusalem to persuade Tonka Greenbaum to give him a divorce. How could he persuade her? I asked. By telling her she was betraying the homeland?

Zionka's mother had come in as usual and listened to the conversation. She said, "There were never any divorces In your family, Miriam. If your sister, may she rest in peace, were alive …" Aunt Miriam cut her off angrily, "My sister was a great patriot."

In the meantime, I had a brilliant idea. A perfect prank. Maybe I would introduce Imri's second wife to the English pilot, so she could steal his heart, and then

Major Parker would break off a branch that a swarm of bees had landed on and give it to her, and he would call her "Toni." In return, she would let him taste her nectar and whisper in his ear, "Charlie." A branch that a swarm of bees had landed on had the power to awaken love? Just an old superstition. Only Zionka could believe nonsense like that.

———

Anna stayed in the house and wrote more letters. I didn't understand what else was left for her to write. Nothing new had happened since she sent the last giant bundle. I started thinking that there were people in the world who write letters to themselves. Maybe Anna hadn't told them she was divorced, because maybe being divorced was not such a great honor in Poland.

When Imri wasn't home, I was in charge. That was a phrase I really liked. I had to get rid of the guns that same night and find a new hiding place. I sprawled on my stomach on my bed, throwing socks at the Jewish National Fund blue box. It was too bad Johnny couldn't help me now. I needed a look-out who could warn me if strangers were around. My dog was recovering from his wound, but it seemed he liked being pampered in my bed, sinking into the soft lace pillows I brought from Aunt Miriam's winter closet, chewing on my shoes to his heart's content. He was still bandaged, but his tail wagged and there was the spark of a smile in his yellow eyes. I told him the details of my plan.

We'll put our heads together. Your doghouse is out of the question, Johnny, because it's too close to the shed. The chickens' water trough is too far, and you know that

Zionka's mother is even worse than the chickens. The only thing left is the dowry trunk that Anna brought from Poland. A perfect hiding place.

I was pleased with myself, and Johnny also barked happily. No one would look there. Certainly not the polite Major Charles Timothy Parker, who called her "Annie."

The blue box was banging against the door, but was still hanging on. I'd thrown all my socks at it, and they fell like the twigs of a tree.

You see, Johnny, that's a sign that I'll be able to get rid of the guns. When Imri comes back, I'll tell him everything, and he'll be proud of how clever I was. Maybe he'll ask me to go on a mission for the homeland too.

It was night. I pretended I was going to sleep. I yawned at the table, and said I was tired. I put on my pajamas, brushed my teeth, and Aunt Miriam was happy. "The *tachseet* is finally on the right track," she said to Anna, who didn't reply. I thought she was anxious to know whether Imri had been able to get rid of Tonka Greenbaum and get a divorce. She wanted to check on Johnny Weissmuller before she went to bed, but I put her off. I didn't want her to see the equipment I had spread out on my bed: the rope, the kerosene lamp, the dark clothes, and I even dug out of my drawer a small dagger Mohammed once gave me. Anna looked dejected, taking my refusal to mean she was no longer needed.

Aunt Miriam consoled her, "Tonya Greenbaum will understand that you cannot hold a man against his will." She said her name as if it were a dirty word.

Then Aunt Miriam shrugged and sighed hopelessly. "Sometimes I think that child is a hopeless case. What will I tell his mother?" That was how she admitted to Anna that she talked to my mother every day. I thought Anna would be shocked, the way she had been before, and would think that my aunt had gone completely crazy. But Anna accepted her words calmly, as if conversations with dead people were perfectly natural.

I waited for them to fall asleep. Johnny Weissmuller was snoring on my bed. Spittle was dripping from his mouth onto Aunt Miriam's lace pillow.

I was lying on my back in my clothes, my hands folded behind my head, staring into the darkness. I loved the night, not sleep, which I thought was a waste of time. I slept the best when it started getting light, and then it was hard for Aunt Miriam to wake me up. Every morning, she threatened to throw cold water on me from the washtub.

Some people are afraid of the night, like Zionka, for example. She dreamed that something terrible was happening to her father, who paved roads. Now she had a new nightmare of Nazis screaming "Jews, get out!" and she woke up covered in sweat. Maybe I'll ask our teacher to reassure her.

My favorite time was when everybody was drifting around in his own world. Then I was wide awake, and thought up my best pranks. If they would teach me how to read and write at night, then maybe I would learn something, although now, after I saw a movie, I knew that you could make up stories without knowing even a single letter.

It was totally dark. I was piloting a Nimrod Hawker straight into the Beit Ha'Am Cinema, landing inside the screen. Just me. Imri wasn't with me, and before morning came, I would get to see lots of movies. That boosted my spirits, because it was a sign that I still had lots of things to accomplish in my life.

Chapter 19

Everything was going according to plan. I slid down the rope. Maybe I could be a movie actor too. Cheetah's part would be a cinch for me. In fact, I'd be willing to play any part at all.

I didn't need a light because the night air was filled with hovering fireflies, a sure sign that spring was on its way. I opened the toolshed door but didn't turn on the kerosene lamp. After all, Johnny Weissmuller does everything in the dark too.

Effortlessly, I pushed aside Grandfather's clay pots, opened the small door and removed the pistols from the old beehive, working as if I were blind. I didn't fumble because the picture was clear to me, even in the dark. If my teacher could see me now, maybe he would excuse me from reading and writing forever.

I covered the small door with some chicken coop netting I had hidden behind the castor tree before supper, and with Zionka's baby carriage that I had dragged over for camouflage. It had been lying around their yard for years because her mother and father hoped they would have another baby, but I didn't think there was any chance of that now.

I topped the pile of junk with the shoes Johnny had

chewed up this week and the old clothes Imri had taken out of my father's valise before his first trip to Europe. Aunt Miriam refused to give away my mother's clothes, even though she never wore them, rejecting the rabbi's appeals to donate them to charity. He said that twelve and a half years had already passed, but Aunt Miriam explained that she couldn't part with them. My birthday is never a happy day, because it's the day we visit my mother's grave.

It was done. Now no one would suspect that guns had been hidden here. Just a run-down old shed packed full of all the things we didn't need but couldn't part with.

But I had something else to hide. I remembered it only after I thought I'd finished. I had to move everything and start all over. I opened the small door again and hid the candlestick I had taken from Anna's trunk in the old beehive, in place of the pistols. If that nosy Englishman should happen to get in here, he'll think it's a family heirloom we've hidden from thieves. I put the three shillings I'd saved up that year next to the candlestick so that Major Parker would be convinced this was the place we stored our valuables. The way Aunt Miriam puts aside *pfuntim*, sterling, for my future education in a respectable profession. I don't know, Aunt Miriam, if they teach how to make movies. I wish I could learn that instead of reading and writing. I felt a twinge of regret about the shillings, because I had planned to spend them on the new Johnny Weissmuller movie coming soon to Tel Aviv, but I consoled myself that something would happen before the sequel to Tarzan arrived. Maybe the English would leave. I absolutely refused to think about the possibility that Anna might have to go.

I was satisfied. True, I hadn't returned the stolen candlestick to Anna, but only because I couldn't yet write the word "sorry."

I climbed into her room through the open window. The curtain billowed across my face. I froze. Darkness suddenly overwhelmed me. The fireflies had vanished and all the objects in the room had been swallowed up. I couldn't even make out the trunk. I tried to recall what Johnny Weissmuller did when faced with an unexpected obstacle, but there hadn't been any scenes like that in the movie.

I began crawling, feeling my way along the floor, praying that Anna wouldn't wake up. I reached the trunk containing her dowry, raised the cover and felt around among the clothes that were no longer neatly arranged the way they had been the day she arrived. I dug down, my fingers touching the hands of a clock. She had shoved the fur coat down to the bottom of the trunk. I ran my fingers over it. Soft and pleasant. I had no idea what kind of an animal it had once been. Not a brown dog, I hoped. I shoved the pistols into the coat sleeves. The coat swelled up, the trunk overflowed, and I was left with two guns I couldn't squeeze in.

The curtain rustled. Suddenly, the darkness dissolved and I saw that Anna's bed was empty. Where had she gone in the middle of the night? I didn't think she could be writing letters in the hen house. For a minute, I was afraid she might have gone off forever, without a goodbye, without a kind word. Maybe she was fed up with lighting a single candle on Friday nights and suffering the pangs of longing and guilt.

Whenever I feel that way, I turn off the kerosene light in my mind and tell myself that my father's heart will not suddenly start beating again, and my mother will never come back into the world through the air. Sometimes I rewind the pictures to the time when they were here, and I feel a little better. There are lots of pictures missing, as if someone had cut them out. My mother died while giving birth to me, so I don't remember her at all, only my father, but even that's something.

I hid behind the curtain, one foot outside, the other propped up against the window sill, and the pistols shoved inside my shirt. Then I heard them, soft voices like the buzzing of a swarm of bees taking off for a blossoming field. They were on Imri's straw mattress, near the door to the room. Anna was leaning diagonally across it. I heard the rustle of falling material. I saw a white hand burst out of a sleeve, a round shoulder peek out and a dress fall to the side. Imri was also undressing. I guessed that she was unbuttoning his shirt, and they were eating something the whole time. Imri whispered, "It's sweet, Anna."

I wanted to turn on a light, but then they would have discovered me. Maybe the fireflies had conspired to help me see what I knew was not meant for my eyes. I was playing the most terrible prank of all, and I couldn't stop. It was playing itself. I was frozen, unmoving, slowly breathing in the darkness. The air was scorching. Maybe I was cold, maybe hot.

Imri removed the pins, one after the other, from Anna's hair. I heard the clink they made when they hit the floor.

He freed her hair, which tumbled down in waves to cover her back. She always wore it up, and now I discovered that it reached below her waist. I saw her from the back, sitting like an erect, white statue. Imri bent and kissed the hollow of her throat, caressed the round lines painted on her skin by the light, holding in his hand an object that glowed in the dark.

"My queen bee," Imri whispered, and I sprang back, almost plummeting from the window sill.

The picture came to me sharp and clear. There was no one to block it. He slipped a honeycomb into her mouth and they both ate from it, each one separately, then both at the same time, the wax cells of the workers and the queen linking them, and again they sucked the honey from the comb, or licked it from each other's skin. Then they seemed to melt as they sank together onto the straw mattress near the door to the room. Now Imri was licking her fingers, then sucking the honeycomb, placing it between her lips like a female worker feeding the queen. But Imri was not a female worker, he was male, and I knew what happened to a male after it mated with the queen. He was doomed. Imri, Imri, you're in more danger than I am. Guns are easier to get rid of than an extra wife. Anna is nothing to you anymore. How come that when you were married, you slept apart, and now, now that you're divorced and married to another woman, you sleep together?

My finger touched the trigger of the pistol. If I were to shoot, they would stop, but the pictures continued to roll. There was nothing that could halt their caresses now, or the gentle buzzing emanating from their throats.

The honeycomb had been tossed aside, and they looked like one person. Her hand, or his, wandered every which way, touching everywhere, and I couldn't tell where her body began and his ended.

"Anna," Imri whispered, "Repeat after me, *ani ohevet otcha*, I love you."

She repeated the words in Hebrew, without the slightest hint of a Polish accent, as if she had been born in Eretz Israel.

Imri

A woman creates life inside her body, and a man cradles it outside her so it will not be spilled, heaven forbid. But I still don't know how to give life, Anna, and I'm afraid to take what is not legally mine.

I feel your longing pouring out of you when you touch the empty hangers in the closet, and I tremble. I have no words, Anna. I don't know how to console you. I search for words you will understand. You teach me to read your body, and yet there is something hidden inside you, a place I cannot reach. Even if you were my wife now, you would remain free. I am not sure if you will ultimately choose me. At first, I thought someone was deceiving me, but now, when I am another woman's husband, I know that it is myself I am deceiving. I promised to marry four women, but I was never required to love.

You walk through the rooms, Anna, and your light steps make the air quiver. I hide my face against your throat, breathe you into me and whisper. My mother said to me, "This is life." I didn't know back then that it was the last time I would hear her voice. My mother's big belly, something fluttering inside, seeking to emerge. If I had known what was going to happen, I would have snatched my hand away and shouted, "This is death!"

I could not save her. The child is not guilty. Stay, Anna.

Chapter 20

Sucking honey. Sucking honey. Sucking honey. I ran, talking to myself. Once, years ago, I swallowed a whole honeycomb and then vomited up my guts. I could feel the sweetness for days. Since then, I've been careful.

The fireflies were chasing me, glittering like the necklace Zionka's mother wore around her neck when she went to a concert in Tel Aviv. And I was getting angry, because even though the tiny lights were beautiful—I admit it—they were only letters the female insects were sending out to the males, and that was a sign language I didn't want to understand.

I had dropped from the window sill with a bang. I wanted to interrupt them, but they kept right on doing what they were doing. Maybe it was something people couldn't stop once they started. I think I was angrier at myself than I was at them.

I had no one to talk to, and anyhow, no one would understand. I knew what a man and a woman did when they were alone, and they didn't do it just to obey the biblical commandment to be fruitful and multiply, like the rabbi said. My mother and father did it, that's a fact—after all, I was born, and so was Imri, twelve years before that. Maybe they were doing it in heaven too.

For their sake, I hoped so, because dead people can't get divorced.

The scene on the screen changed. Jane walked right up to Tarzan, who was a complete stranger, put an arm around his neck and stroked his naked chest, and that was even before he had said a single human word to her.

I corrected myself. It was the actress who was clinging to Johnny Weissmuller. She was just playing a part. What you see in a movie is "fictitious." A stone pulled at my heart, because although Anna and Imri weren't married on paper any more, what I saw wasn't fictitious.

I wanted to stretch out on the ground that was already covered with soft spring grass, and hide from the world, but I had two of the newest made-in-Poland Radom pistols in my shirt that I had to hide, or else, disaster.

I ran and ran. I'd already circled the house ten times, and every time, the curtain billowed in the open window, because curtains had no idea what they were concealing. Even if I pulled it down and ripped it to pieces, they would stay inside and keep on doing what they were doing. And how would it end?

That's what was going through the mind of the marathon runner as every step brought his life closer to its end. I didn't know if he'd known from the beginning that he was going to die a minute before he announced the victory. My teacher didn't say whether they mourned him, or, because of the celebration, they forgot all about him and no one bothered to come to his funeral.

What did they say to each other after they took off their clothes and were naked? I guess there were no secrets then.

I didn't know if Imri sometimes thought about his father and mother, who were also my father and mother. He never mentioned them, as if they had never existed. When Aunt Miriam talked to the air, Imri ignored it. Maybe now, at this very minute, he was telling Anna what hurt him and who he missed, and he was close to her, closer even than he was to me, closer than to any other living soul in the world.

I wanted to sleep. I wanted not to remember. I wished I could think I had gone into a movie theater and seen the wrong movie by mistake. I hadn't meant for it to happen. I wanted somebody to believe me. God, I wanted to *say* I'm sorry, because I still didn't know how to write it.

My father was a beekeeper. My grandfather was a beekeeper. I will never be a beekeeper. I'm going to make movies.

I was so young when it happened that I didn't listen to the warnings. I remember my father yelling "Don't touch!!!" but I still opened the cover of the hive. I didn't know you had to wear a mask. It was the most wonderful feeling in the world—to do what you weren't supposed to do. The bees burst out all at once and stung me all over my body. Sometimes I try to remember the pain, but I can't. I was unconscious for two weeks. I almost died from the bees' poison. Mohammed says that the poison stayed in your body forever, and it actually make you stronger, but I think Mohammed was just trying to make me feel better.

Chapter 21

Light is a spy that sneaks up every morning to check out the territory. First, the closest things are revealed. The house with its tiled roof that Imri hadn't had time to repair since the last rain. The toolshed and the tin shack covered with leaves, and the castor tree that would have to be pruned soon before it spread over the whole yard.

Then the sky becomes completely pale and a gentle mist rises from the earth, like a final yawn. I could see the water tower that overlooked the village, and further away, the English air force base. Barbed wire, pegs and posts, nails and screws. At that silent sunrise time, you could hear the soldiers going out for their morning drill. Our beehives were hidden behind some cypress trees. My grandfather had planted one of them on the day my father was born, but maybe that was just a made-up story too.

From where I was sitting, I could see the Hawkers taking off and landing. Bugs in the sky getting into formation to chase after some unknown nectar. Maybe Major Charles Timothy Parker was at the head of the formation, leading the swarm forward.

Then I started hearing the sounds of the people in the village, waking from their sleep and going to work. Zusia harnessed his horse to the wagon and told his wife to go to the devil; Alter started his van, hurrying the workers to the groves, as if the tangerines were plotting to run away from the trees; and the truck that delivered fresh bread to the villages in the area was parked in front of Aharonchik's bakery. Aharonchik had already managed to tell the driver all the news from the world of the "Truth."

The birds on our trees could wake the dead. That's what Aunt Miriam said. They were so noisy, and because of them, the chickens in our coop were already crowing. Only the Zionist duck in Zionka's yard was still sleeping. It was very tired from the hard work of helping me that night. Even if the English plucked out all its feathers, it wouldn't tell them where the guns were now.

I also heard Johnny Weissmuller barking from my room, looking for me, only to discover that no one had shared his dog dreams that night in my bed.

Early in the morning, that time when no one's fully awake yet, I had taken Anna's stolen candlestick out of its hiding place again, and had rolled it under my bed. Johnny was snoring.

I'd whispered to him, "You know, Johnny, something that has a mate in the world and is still alone, always makes people suspicious."

Now, the whole village was awake. There were sounds coming from Zionka's house too. Zionka was getting dressed. I waited a while on purpose, so I wouldn't catch her without any clothes on, heaven forbid. Whenever Herzl Fleischer came to visit me, he always looked for an excuse to peek into her room from my window. Our string was hanging over my head, and the tin cans on both sides were clattering. Anna said that the telephone reminded her of Chinese wind chimes. I'd love to try the real thing, but they kept the door of the committee house locked, and it was hard to break in through the window.

I was crouched in the same position, unable to move, absorbing the light and watching. I was part of this place, and it was part of me. I knew it so well that sometimes I couldn't really see it, and didn't notice the little details about it, even though I saw them every single day.

I never stopped and looked around, the way I was doing now, to see if there was anything beautiful here, or to tell myself exactly what I loved about this place. What colors there were, and which smells and sounds stirred up a quiet humming inside me—usually the colors and smells and sounds that didn't affect anyone else at all.

This was the only place I would always call "mine," no matter where I was.

I couldn't imagine myself living in some Polish town called Lutsk and feeling the same way.

Now I was curious about what Anna felt when she opened the window in the morning and looked out at all of this, a sight she had seen for the first time only six months ago. I can't believe she called it "mine." How can she feel the way I did?

And maybe I was wrong.

I picked up a stone and threw it at Zionka's window. I was a champion thrower from all my practice with the Jewish National Fund blue box. The stone hit the glass with a thud. Zionka's curls appeared. I signaled her to go to the tin can on her side, and then climbed up the tree that grew on my side. I still wasn't ready to go into the house. I reached inside my window, took the can, and held it next to my mouth, covering half my face, "Hello, Zionka, can you hear me?"

"Uzik, what are you doing outside so early?" Zionka said, surprised, She knew I liked to sleep in the morning.

"Don't ask too many questions. I hid two pistols. In your duck pen, behind the tub."

"What?" Through the can now pressed up against my ear, I heard her swallow a few breaths, and it made the echo louder.

"Don't worry, Zionka, it's for the sake of the homeland."

I quickly took the can away from my ear so the shouting wouldn't make me deaf. Zionka always shouted when she was scared.

"Uzik, come down immediately!"

Aunt Miriam was shaking her fist at me. She looked really menacing this time. I slid down quickly, landing like a sack of potatoes, and I could feel the scratches on my knees.

"Since when are you so conscientious, getting up so early for school?" Aunt Miriam had a special sense that told her when a prank was being played.

I said I'd gone outside for some fresh air, that I didn't feel well, and she immediately put her hand on my forehead and ordered me to open my mouth. In the end, Aunt Miriam had no choice but to believe me, but she grumbled quietly, "He probably has a reading test he wants to get out of."

Anna was in the kitchen. Again, I looked at her through the window. Her back was to me, but now she was dressed. All her buttons were buttoned and her hair was again rolled into a bun on the back of her neck. She was arranging the eggs she had gathered that morning in a pail. It was strange that I hadn't seen her go out to the hen house. I'd been outside all night.

Anna was so startled when I threw open the door that she dropped an egg. She knelt down and scrubbed the floor hard to get rid of the sticky egg white and the yolk. She didn't say a word, not even "Good morning." She was mute again. Maybe she'd used up all her words at night. The poison in me was coming to life. That white back, the curves of that body and those hands that touched and caressed, his body, her body, to suck honey ...

Enough! Enough already! I heard myself screaming inside.

Anna stood up. I saw that her eyes were red and swollen. My anger had its own voice. It would be good for beekeepers to get stung once. You had to pay a price, and I sounded to myself like one of the agitators who stirred up the people in Mohammed's village. Nectar for nectar—poison for poison. There was the taste of spoiled honey in my mouth. If this was what happened after a man and women slept together, I was not going to get married. Not even "fictitiously."

I raced up to my room and threw myself down onto the straw carpet Mohammed and Fahtma had given me on my birthday once when we came back from the cemetery. Johnny Weissmuller drowned me with slobbery licks.

Imri knocked on my door and came in without waiting for my permission. "I came to say goodbye. I'm going away again. What're you doing on the floor?"

My anger was raging. I didn't want to answer.

Imri knelt down. Just the way he had at night. Except that I wasn't Anna.

"Won't you give me a hug, little brother?"

You don't have any hugs left, Imri. You gave them all to Anna.

I avoided him by rolling over on the carpet.

"You're going to get married again?" I asked. "Aren't two wives enough for you? Do you have to write a third wife's name in your passport? You'll be famous all over the world. Even more than Johnny Weissmuller. The man who got married more times than anyone else."

"You'll understand when you're grown up, little brother."

I rolled around again, and kicked him, as if by accident. I wouldn't understand more later on than I did now. Grown up. It sounded like a dirty word.

I said, "Did you manage to get divorced last night? Did you get a divorce on your straw mattress, or did you give one, it's so confusing …"

Imri looked so fresh and healthy. Nature had gone crazy. The male bee was saved, and it was the queen who was hurt.

He sat down on the carpet near me, plucking off pieces of straw.

"I want to tell you a secret. Swear to me you won't tell anyone. I trust you, Uzik. I'm not going to Europe to get married. That's not the real reason. I'm going to buy weapons for the Jews in our homeland."

"You're not going to sell our honey?"

"No. You're right to be angry at me."

I said, "So many lies."

Imri tried to hug me. My body was rigid.

"We have a weapons cache in the village. I can't tell you where. Not because I don't trust you, little brother, but because I don't want to put you in danger. What you don't know can't hurt you."

"And what about the things you do know?"

Imri didn't answer.

I said, "I wish it could all be erased."

Your cache, Imri, is not mine. Only I and the Zionist duck know where the weapons are really hidden.

He promised this would be his last trip. He said he made that promise to Anna too, and when he said her name, his eyes glowed. Everything would be different when he came back, he said.

But I wouldn't give in. "Sweet words. Why should I believe you? After all, you do everything 'fictitiously'."

Imri didn't get insulted. He pulled me to him as hard as he could. I almost choked.

"I understand you, little brother. Alone with Aunt Miriam … it's hard …"

I interrupted, "I'm not alone!"

He looked under my bed.

"So you have a cache too," Imri pinched me affectionately as he looked at the blue box on the door and the socks piled on top of it. He liked my target. He pulled a dirty sock from under my bed and hurled it at the box with all his strength, but he wasn't a champion.

Instead of hitting the target, he knocked the box off the nail.

"I hope Johnny Weissmuller gets well. And make sure he doesn't cross any fences to run after English females," he said.

And I replied quietly, "Or Polish ones."

Imri stood up. I stayed lying on the carpet. I didn't have the strength to lift a finger. From my crooked angle, I could see the rope and the candlestick under the bed. I didn't know if Imri had seen them. He just got up and left.

Chapter 22

The rabbi said that because Tonka Greenbaum refused to give her husband a divorce, he had to find a way for them to get divorced against her will. Maybe because he liked Anna, or maybe because Tonka's refusal was a disgrace to the homeland. I had a few clever pranks I could have suggested, but Anna refused to cooperate. She said that no one had the right to interfere. Imri and Tonka had decided to get married of their own free will, so they also had to decide themselves to get divorced.

The rabbi mumbled, "And sometimes we have to help a bit. A little push, and all the problems are solved, right Uziel?"

Mohammed was lucky, rabbi. He could be married to four women at the same time. If the English ever decided to put a quota on the Arabs coming to Palestine, Mohammed could actually enter the names of four wives in his passport, for the sake of the homeland. One of these days, I'd have to find out once and for all if Mohammed's homeland is the same as mine.

Aunt Miriam was pouring tea for the rabbi again, the kind he liked. I'd once secretly put a few leaves from Fahtma's garden into the kettle, and the rabbi had praised the tea so much that Aunt Miriam blushed. She took a jewelry box out of the closet and spilled onto the table a gold bracelet, a string of pearls and two wedding rings. She said to the rabbi, "This is my sister's jewelry, may she rest in peace. Give it to that woman in exchange for a divorce," and she didn't mention Tonka Greenbaum's name.

The rabbi sighed and pushed away the jewelry. Aunt Miriam shoved the jewelry in Anna's direction, saying that she had taken the wedding rings from my mother's finger before she was buried. I was seven hours old then, and no one expected me to remember her. Sometimes, though, I thought I did remember something. Crawling through a dark tunnel towards a place flooded with light, hearing a great shriek, and then silence.

I had no idea why Aunt Miriam had never sucked honey. She'd never gotten married, not even once, for the sake of the homeland, or even for her own sake. Once, I heard her tell my mother in the air that Zusia the wagoner deserved a better wife than the one he had.

Anna returned the jewelry to the box, arranging it gently and placing my mother's wedding ring next to my father's. I didn't remember them taking my father's ring off his finger after his heart stopped beating. I had no idea how far back my memory went.

"Some day, Uzik, you'll give them to your wife as a gift, " Anna said as she closed the box.

I don't plan to get married, Anna. Even if Zionka begs me. Because if we have a baby, she might die. How lucky the bees were. After their male dies, the newborn is left with lots of mothers.

Imri's queen had become an ordinary worker bee.

The day after he left, Anna scrubbed the house from top to bottom. I thought she might be suffering from sugar poisoning, a disease that attacks people who suck too much honey. Maybe Imri was also suffering from it now, shaving on the deck of a ship on the way to Europe, humming stupid songs to the empty sky. I felt relieved. The rabbi said that God created man in his own image, "Male and female He created them and blessed them," but I knew that Anna would be saved. For the time being, the danger had passed.

Anna polished all the brass objects in the cabinet. No one had touched them in years. She straightened out all the closets, except for the closet where my mother's clothes still hung. She washed out the hen house, threatening to douse the chickens, and she even watered the castor tree, which didn't need water at all. The toolshed was the only place I wouldn't let her into.

Aunt Miriam asked her what was so urgent, and Anna said that she had to get everything done. She had to fulfill all her duties before …

"Before what?"

"You have to learn to at least write my name, Uzik. It's so simple. Only four letters."

"What for?"

"So that if I'm far away some day, you'll be able to recognize the letter I send you and open it."

I whispered, "It's a waste of time," but Anna insisted. She took my hand in hers and walked it along the page. The pencil shook. I wanted to stop. Anna, don't force me. If you made that second wife practice writing one word for a whole day, Tonka Greenbaum would finally surrender and beg to give Imri a divorce.

Aunt Miriam reported to the air that Imri had gone away again. She was still hiding the fact that there was a second wife, maybe so as not to worry my mother, who was liable to think that, with so many daughter-in-laws, she wouldn't have any grandchildren. God created the male and the female. I would've liked to have a few words with God, blessed be His name, about that prank of His, separating the sexes.

I just hoped that no baby would be born. It would have two mothers, and wouldn't know which was the real one. A child with two mothers is just as bad as a child who has no mother at all. A child is a dangerous thing altogether, Johnny. It could kill its mother without meaning to.

But if there was a child, would I be its uncle? I wasn't sure I liked the idea of being someone's "Aunt Miriam." Johnny Weissmuller, tell me please, whether Tarzan and Jane have a child in the next movie.

If our winter was in a movie, we wouldn't suffer from the cold. Even when terrible things happened in a movie, I felt safe and protected. Harry the hunter's shot didn't kill Tarzan. If it had, the movie would have ended too soon and the audience would have gotten mad. The people who made movies knew you couldn't replace Johnny Weissmuller with someone else.

We'd sat in the third row in the Beit Ha'Am. Imri said mockingly that it wasn't a real theater, just four walls made of wooden planks around a large open area. He also saw mice scurrying around among the squeaky wooden chairs. He'd suggested that we go across the street to the Gan Rina cinema, where it was much more pleasant in the summer, but "Tarzan, King of the Apes" was only playing in Beit Ha'Am.

At first, I wanted to sit in the front row, but Imri objected. It wasn't good to sit too close, he said. I argued with him. and remained sitting alone facing the screen. But the minute the lights went off, I hurried back to sit next to him, only because I still didn't know what to expect in that unfamiliar darkness.

The trees in the movies looked very tall. It was hard to believe that a person could climb them. Imri laughed and said that what I saw wasn't what was really there. If I had known the word then, I would have said it was a "fictitious" jungle. Cardboard trees, paper leaves, and Johnny Weissmuller used a ladder to get to the top, just the way I did, only they didn't film that. An old man sitting behind us scolded Imri, telling him to be quiet. I was jealous of you, Imri. You'd already seen lots of movies in your life. Too bad you never had the time to tell me about all of them.

It was raining in the movie, and the large drops sounded like drumbeats. But even so, I was completely dry, waiting for the downpour to end, the way we were waiting for Imri now. I sat there calmly, even at the most suspenseful moments of the movie, because I knew that soon, in a minute, an hour, maybe more—they would overcome all the obstacles. In the dark, it seemed possible to move time around. Except that sometimes, I was sorry I couldn't get inside the head of the person who made the movie to really find out what would happen. Imri said I was in for a few surprises. Even if you plan every little thing, nothing happens they way you want it to.

That kid. That kid. We heard whispering behind us. A few other angry people had joined the old man. "Take the kid out!" The usher bent down to us and asked, "Is that your child?"

Imri said yes, and took my hand.

Johnny Weissmuller roared, and I roared with him.

The Rabbi

Man must prepare for the coming of the Messiah by giving birth to all the souls that were meant to be born. Those who are not fruitful and do not multiply delay the coming of the Messiah. I will proclaim that publicly in our synagogue, Miriam, for even after the Bar Kokhba uprising, the Jews of Eretz Israel were required to strictly observe the commandment to multiply and be fruitful in order to increase their numbers. This is all the more necessary in this time of the second return to Zion.

If the world was created by the Almighty, may His name be blessed, then nothing that has been created is ugly or worthless. Adam and Eve were not ashamed of their nakedness, because their reproductive organs were like eyes or hands, parts of their body.

The mating between Anna and Imri was not a mockery. If they were married in the presence of witnesses, their marriage is sanctified in all respects, and it can be nullified only by a formal divorce. He is divorced and she is divorced. There is nothing to be done about it, and whatever they did, if they did, was permitted by God, may His name be blessed, for only a short period of time.

Our mentor, Rabbi Avraham Itzhak Kook wisely reminded us that we are just as much flesh as we are holy spirit. Man is forbidden to be alone, and I, Miriam, am not Ben-Azai, that most well-known bachelor in the Talmud. His friends attacked him for preaching the need to have offspring, while he himself remained an ascetic. He countered their attack by saying, "And what can I do if my soul desires the Torah?"

My soul desires the Torah, but I also wish to fulfill the commandment. Come, Miriam, let us both follow the wisdom of Rabbi Kook, for the weakened soul will be illuminated by the power of the sanctified flesh.

Chapter 23

"The dog is staying home," Aunt Miriam declared firmly. Johnny Weissmuller stared at her with his moist eyes, but she didn't back down.

I tried to console him. An emergency meeting at the village committee house would be very frustrating for a dog. Everyone is tense and excited and carries on about the common enemy, and you, Johnny, will want to attack him, only to find that the enemy is somewhere else.

Aunt Miriam said to me, "When will you learn that dogs do not understand what you say to them?" and I muttered into Johnny's fur, how does my aunt know that dead people understand better?

I still made an effort to explain to him that the meeting of the elected officials of the Hebrew community had declared it a legal holiday for everyone in protest against the cutback in the number of immigrants. That obviously had nothing to do with him, because dogs never change their habits and would never be new immigrants, but something else happened that is bothering me, Johnny, I whispered to him. Smuggled guns were found in a shipment of barrels of cement that arrived in Jaffa, and members of the Arab delegation were demanding that the English step up their searches.

It was really was a state of emergency, Johnny. How lucky you are that you don't dream. Last night, Zionka had a nightmare that woke her up. She saw herself being killed instead of the Jewish sergeant Moshe Rosenfeld from Kibbutz Ein Harod, who was shot by the gang of Arab raiders, called the Az a-Din el-Kasam. Zionka refused to go to the meeting, and nothing I said about a nightmare being only a nightmare helped.

At first, Aunt Miriam had been surprised that I was willing to go with her and Anna, but she didn't hide how happy she was, because she thought it was a sign that I was starting to be "fixed." That's what Anna told me.

Fixing things, Johnny. How can you fix a torn film? I don't know how to paste it together. It happened twice in the Beit Ha'Am. Most of the people in the audience gave up the second time and got their money back. Imri wanted to leave too, but I insisted we stay, and after a short break, they really did start to show the movie again. To this day, I'm not sure if a scene wasn't missing. I'll have to see the movie again, Johnny, and not only for that reason.

—

In the middle of the meeting, when the committee chairman slammed his fist down on the table, his face red with excitement, and announced the steps that had to be taken, because "They shall not prevail," I left the hall and tiptoed through the towards the chairman's room, where the telephone was. A real telephone, a telephone I had never dialed, and already, the whole conversation was running through my mind.

"The Bristol Garden Guest House?"

I would ask them to call Miss Tonka Greenbaum to the telephone. She was staying there, a new immigrant from Poland. You couldn't miss her. She was wearing the latest fashions from Paris.

Who is calling?

Her "fictitious" brother-in-law.

And I would tell her that she had to go away and leave us alone. No one had taken the marriage seriously. Listen, Tonka Greenbaum, sometimes things happen backwards in life. Sometimes a couple that really intended to get married discovers after the ceremony that the marriage was "fictitious."

And I had another argument to convince her. If marriage was such a great thing, why didn't the Almighty, may His name be blessed, create a mate for himself out of His rib? What else could I say to her that would convince her to divorce Imri? Believe me, Tonka Greenbaum, you'll find better men than Imri in Eretz Israel. Taller, better looking men, who know how to dance the tango and who go to the movies not only as a favor to their younger brothers. You have no idea how much I had to beg him to take me. Meir, the charming butcher, could be an ideal husband for you.

The door to the committee chairman's room was open. The telephone was beckoning to me. It was exactly the way I imagined it. Its dial was gleaming, and silvery numbers completed the picture. I was so excited. I pulled a Players I'd stolen from Imri out of my pocket and pushed it between my dry lips. The old tobacco was falling out of it, but the cigarette made me feel stronger. Imri said he liked to see movies alone. He dragged along behind me to Tel Aviv last summer against his will. Only because Aunt Miriam ordered him to, and he always obeyed Aunt Miriam's orders. He also said he got the greatest kick out of sneaking into a movie theater. Why pay if you can get it free? What could I offer you in exchange for a divorce, Tonka Greenbaum? A Jewish National Fund blue box full of coins, and a dog, that was all I owned in the world. And I would never give away Johnny Weissmuller.

I picked up the receiver, heard a sharp sound, and then the operator asked what number I wanted to call. I opened my mouth and the cigarette fell onto the floor. This was no tin can on the end of a string connecting only Zionka and me. I could talk to the whole world from this telephone. "Hello, hello, Miss Operator, do you know how to call Johnny Weissmuller in Hollywood?"

"Johnny Weissmuller? You idiot, don't you know that movies are pure lies?"

That wasn't the voice of the operator. Herzl Fleischer was standing behind me, laughing. He had followed me. Excited voices were coming from the hall. The voting had started. Herzl Fleischer knocked the receiver out of my hand. Wrapped in the wire, it fell to the floor, the operator's voice coming out of it, irritable or frustrated, "Hello, hello."

Herzl Fleischer punched me in the face. I touched my cheek, and my fingers were covered in blood.

"I'll tell everyone," Herzl yelled, "and when they expel you, Zionka will be mine."

Chapter 24

Darkness again. Something is wrong with the movie. The hallway filled with the sound of people walking and I knew the emergency meeting was over. I managed to put the receiver back in its cradle and run outside. Herzl Fleischer had disappeared.

I grabbed the matchbox, stolen with Imri's Players, lit the cigarette, inhaled the smoke mixed with blood and choked. Two guys were waiting for me at the back of the committee house. I recognized them immediately. They were the ones from the van. Although I didn't like them and didn't know their names, I walked towards them because I hoped they had some news from Imri. Was Lutsk close to the city of Radom, where they made the guns? I didn't dare ask Anna.

The tall one pointed to me and said, "You should do something for the sake of the homeland too."

The homeland demanded too much, I thought, saying, " I'm only twelve and a half, and you can't get married at this age."

The short one burst out laughing. "A smart kid, a real beekeeper. He already smokes cigarettes, and now he wants to get a taste of women. Are you interested in airplanes too? We want you to sniff around the English base. No one'll suspect you. After all, you don't even know how to read and write."

In the distance, I saw Zionka walking towards the committee house. Soon, the people would be coming out and she would disappear in the crowd. I wanted to run to her, but the tall guy blocked the way.

"Bees lose their way. You can say you got lost chasing after Hawkers. You know how to count, don't you, or do you have a problem with that too?"

I stopped trying to get past them.

"The British have storerooms full of weapons. You report to us when the sentries change shifts at the gate, and how many military policemen walk around the base at night."

The tall one bent down to me. I saw Zionka walking along the path and Herzl Fleischer walking towards her. "Ask him," I pointed to Herzl Fleischer, "He'd be happy to do something for the sake of something."

The tall one said to his friend, "The kid's not as innocent as he looks." And then he said to me, "Do you know why your brother goes to Europe?"

"I don't give away secrets."

The short one tapped the tall one on the arm. "A model of loyalty, a tough guy with principles." He was making fun of me. He was using Mohammed's fancy words, but I felt that he meant just the opposite.

Herzl Fleischer put his arm around Zionka's shoulders. My cheek, where he had punched it, was swelling up. I pressed all my fingers up against the pain. The blood had clotted. Zionka would tell him about her nightmare and he would promise to protect her. There was a huge collection of guns from all periods of history in his house.

The tall guy wanted to leave. "I told you the boy wasn't the right person," he explained to his friend. "They say in the village that he's wild and lazy. He can't learn anything. He can't be trusted."

Zionka and Herzl Fleischer looked like two dots disappearing in the distance. I couldn't see whether she had put her arm around his shoulders.

The short guy wouldn't give up. He lowered his face to my ear and whispered, "We'll talk to your teacher about not keeping you down a grade. It'll be worth your while. Your brother won't have to travel any more. We'll fill our storerooms with weapons. Do it for his sake and not for the sake of the homeland."

I wanted to yell that the homeland was a joke. I'll try really hard. I'll write the sentence a hundred times, without Zionka's help, until my hand aches.

Even though I ran after Zionka and Herzl Fleischer, I didn't catch up to them. They were too fast. The kids said he would skip a grade at the end of the year. I sat on the ground. The cigarette fell apart before I could smoke it to the end. Imri wanted to smoke in the movies, but the usher wouldn't let him. When I asked Anna to tell me about the movies in Poland, she argued with me. She said she preferred books, and tried to convince me that what the eye doesn't see is a thousand times more powerful. In a book, Anna said, you can even turn yourself into an animal. A dog, perhaps. And your Tarzan, she said, could be tall or short, with black curly hair like Imri's, or golden hair like Meir the butcher's, and you could even make the roar so loud in your mind that it would be deafening.

Anna hadn't see Tarzan. She only knew Shirley Temple, the little girl who danced and sang, and the dog Rin Tin Tin, and the western movies where the white men fought the Indians and the cowboys shot each other in gunfights. Even though Anna didn't like those kinds of movies, I thought I would really enjoy them.

For whose sake did Johnny Weissmuller do what he did? I had a feeling that if he roared for anyone's sake, then it had to be the person watching the movie. And maybe it was for me.

Zionka, I yelled, wait for me, but the path was empty.

Zionka's Mother

As his teacher, you should have him sent to an institution. That's your duty as an educator. It's a hard thing to do, but there is no choice. You have to remove the plague before it afflicts us all.

Now that his older brother is in Europe on a mission for the homeland and we don't know whether he'll come back, now is the opportunity to get rid of that boy.

I don't blame anyone, not even poor Miriam who did everything in her power to teach him properly. Who would have thought she'd waste her life that way.

The boy is hopeless, I'm telling you. Socializes with Englishmen and Arabs, and he'll bring disaster down on our heads. He bewitches my Zionka with his pranks. He whispers buttery words from the other side of that string he stretched between our windows.

My husband disagrees with me. He's naive enough to think the boy will surprise us all yet. He only plays pranks so others will feel sorry for him, but I've been watching him from the day he was born and his mother died, and I know he's a lost case.

No one doubts your intelligence. But if you don't do something soon, I won't hesitate to talk to the principal, and I'll even bang on the committee chairman's desk, because there is no place in our community for that little devil.

And in the meantime, separate him from the others, sit him on the left side of the classroom, far from my Zionka. If you want my advice, it would be better if you sat Herzl Fleischer next to her. He's such a talented boy, and we are all amazed at what a gifted collector he is. Someday, he'll be a great leader.

The boy must leave the village. I shudder at the thought that my only daughter might some day have such an illiterate, ignorant husband.

Chapter 25

One morning, when Anna was sweeping and raking dry leaves that had piled up in our yard over the winter, the photographer who took pictures in all the villages of the area arrived, leading an old horse carrying a huge camera on its back. Someone had sent him, the photographer wouldn't say who. He'd heard there was a young, recently married couple here. He was offering a family picture at a special price, boasting that only he included second and third cousins in his frame, because his camera has a wide lens, the most modern lens there was, like a movie camera. Even neighbors, or "family friends" might find themselves in the picture.

Anna offered the photographer a deal. He could photograph her whole family, which included her mother and father, her little sister, all her sisters- and brothers-in-law and nieces and nephews, and she explained who was related to whom, a long, complicated list. The photographer's eye glittered and his nose quivered, because he smelled a fat fee. Anna didn't leave out a single member of her tribe. She just neglected to mention a small detail—they were all in Poland.

In exchange for letting him take this family picture with his modern camera, she asked the photographer to lend her his scrawny horse for one day. That was how I found out, to my surprise, that Anna was a really good rider.

"A horse," I asked, puzzled. "What do you need a horse for?" And I started suspecting that lonely people, like Aunt Miriam, looked for strange things to occupy their time.

Without a second thought, the photographer shook her hand, and the deal was made. Anna patted the horse, helped me up, and jumped onto its back behind me.

"You said to the Englishman ..."

"What I said to the Englishman doesn't matter." She slapped the horse's back and galloped forward.

We rode to Mohammed's village to buy new queen bees. That kind of visit to his village always meant the beginning of spring. Anna said it was the last duty she had to fulfill. I didn't want to ruin her illusion by telling her that the duties have to be fulfilled every day all over again. And besides, I was very happy to be visiting Mohammed, who we hadn't seen since Johnny Weissmuller was wounded.

I was sitting in front of Anna, her hair flying in the wind, slapping against my ears, and I showed her the way to the village. The road wound between the hills, and the old horse's hooves raised dust.

I pointed to the terraced hills covered with vineyards, to the ancient olive trees with their silver-gray leaves, and the tomb of the Sheik, who the Jews also considered a holy man. People came to his grave to make wishes. I'd made some wishes too, when I visited with Mohammed, and I was still waiting for the Sheik to grant them.

A herd of goats was skidding down the hillside, blocking the entrance to the village. We heard the muezzin calling the people to prayers from the minaret of the mosque. I pointed to him and explained to Anna that you had to take off your shoes before going into a Moslem holy place, and that even in the middle of a workday, when he was covered from head to toe in his beekeeper's suit, Mohammed turned in the direction of Mecca, knelt on the ground and prayed.

We waited for the goats to pass, leaving behind their droppings and the echoes of their bleating, moving slowly, as if they had all the time in the world. We weren't in a hurry either. Anna said the countryside was so different that you might think we'd arrived in another country by mistake. She held me tight, as if, for a minute, she'd confused me with Imri. At first, my body was rigid, and the poison deep inside me was still seething. Her hair smelled of honey. I hadn't known how intoxicating it was. She was like a new queen bee, and it was hard to explain to Anna why a new queen bee had to be crowned every spring.

"And you, Anna, who do you love?"

"In the movies or in real life?" she asked, replying immediately, "Clark Gable," and I was disappointed.

I asked Anna to whisper soft words in the horse's ear, and she whispered something in Polish. I was disappointed again. I thought she'd managed to learn a soft word or two in Hebrew, and she said she wasn't sure whether the word she'd said was soft or harsh.

"Tell me, Anna, and I'll decide. I've already learned a few words in Polish from you."

She didn't answer me.

"Imri trusts me!" I said.

That melted her. She leaned over and whispered the word in my ear. I heard it clearly, as if she were talking to me on a real telephone. And it wasn't Zionka who was whispering. I couldn't repeat that complicated Polish word. If she said what I thought she did, then the word was short and simple in Hebrew. I thought Anna had said "love."

Chapter 26

"Stop! Stop!"

One minute, the village was quiet and peaceful, dozing in the afternoon warmth that was the first sign of the hot summer to come. Only donkeys could be seen grazing on the grass in the yards, because the people of the village were resting in their houses. And the next minute, a gang of older boys on horseback was standing in front of us, their faces hidden by kaffiyehs, pistols and daggers in their belts.

These gangs, the *shabab*, usually dared to come out only at night. During the day, they were afraid the English would chase them down. This was the first time I'd seen them in the daytime. I didn't always believe Aunt Miriam's horrible stories about all the *goyim* just waiting to kill us. Even Zionka thought Aunt Miriam exaggerated sometimes.

One of them hissed, *Itbach el-Yahud*, kill the Jews.

"What's he saying?" Anna asked.

I didn't want to translate.

"Don't pay any attention, Anna. They're just the *shabab*—a bunch of young men who make a lot of noise. They're not the majority."

The leader of the *shabab* came up to us. Anna sat

erect in the saddle, holding me tightly around the waist. I felt her body tense behind me, her feet in the stirrups, signaling the horse to be ready to take off. Suddenly, we seemed to be in a movie, but I was confused. I didn't know what part I was supposed to be playing.

"Get out of here. This is our land," and even before Anna could reply, we saw Fahtma Daudi running towards us from the end of the narrow street, shouting.

"Don't touch them. They're our guests!"

The leader froze. He looked down at the small figure of Mohammed's sister.

"You lick the boots of the Jews. Tell your brother to stop working for them, and you, foreigner," he spat the words at Anna, "go back to where you came from. Like the cursed locust, you settle on our land, and your numbers grow greater from day to day."

Even though I skipped over the harsh words, Anna understood everything.

"We didn't come to steal anything away from you." Her words in English rang out clearly, because the muezzin had finished calling the people to prayers. "You have your village and we have ours." That was the first time Anna said that something was hers.

The leader spurred his horse, and the rest of the gang did the same, "We burn locusts with fire. And we shall burn you too."

How do westerns end, Anna? Because you don't like those movies, I don't know how they end.

Fahtma took hold of the old horse's bridle and led him gently, cunningly increasing the distance between Anna and the gang leader. Then, she shot her a sidelong glance that implied something about the leader. All of a sudden, he looked to me like a kid dressed up in a costume.

"Men are too hotheaded. They burn in their own fire. I hope you don't grow up to be that way, Aza'ar. If we women had anything to say about it, we would've put out the fire a long time ago, and thrown all the guns and daggers into the sea.

We sat on a mat in the grape arbor in the Daudi family's yard, the almost ripe clusters of grapes dangling above us. The smell of the herbs Fahtma grew in the garden and in the large clay flowerpots filled the air. She picked and gave Anna some mint, coriander, summer savory, saffron, and even bitter wormwood, explaining to her the powers of each herb and which diseases it healed. These were the herbs Fahtma used to make the miracle salve for Johnny Weissmuller.

Mohammed and Fahtma's father came to sit with us, and we sipped sweet coffee from small copper cups. He offered me one too. "A boy protecting the honor of his brother's wife is himself a hero," he said. We finished our first and second cups. I refused the third, because that was the polite thing to do, but I drank it anyway. The fourth I declined with a thank you. Anna followed my lead. Mohammed and Fahtma's father studied her and said, "Our people would pay the good price of a hundred goats for a bride like you."

I translated, and Anna blushed. Fahtma smiled and their eyes met. Her father wanted to marry her to a rich old man from a village in the Galilee, but she was secretly in love with her cousin, Imad, who rode with me and Mohammed when I visited the village.

I said in Hebrew that Imri had gotten her for free, and I didn't add that maybe he was now paying the price for his second wife.

Mohammed taught Anna to tear the pita bread and dip it into the fresh yogurt, and I was gorging myself on olives, filling my pockets with the pits I would later throw at the Jewish National Fund box. I noticed that Anna's legs were folded perfectly under her.

Anna hesitated. "With my hands?" she looked embarrassed, the way Tarzan did in the movie when Jane was teaching him his first words.

Fahtma nodded encouragingly. I thought she was secretly jealous of Anna, who was free to choose her own husband. I thanked God, may His name be blessed, that Aunt Miriam had rejected Zusia the wagoner. Otherwise, he would be living with us and praying for the devil to take me. Anna tore the pita, dipped it and ate it. Her lips glistened from the olive oil.

Mohammed brought the bees in a glass jar that reminded me of the hated crystal ball tossed somewhere in my room.

"Be careful," Mohammed warned us, "the queen is a delicate creature. She started life as an ordinary worker, and now she's suddenly responsible for a whole beehive. Do you remember the word 'responsible', Aza'ar? It's the only one you really must memorize."

To avoid the *shabab*, Mohammed led us to the olive grove on the outskirts of the village. From there, a side road led to our village. As we were saying goodbye, he warned us not to stray to the left or right of it.

Anna curtseyed to him, saying, "The gray-eyed girl thanks you, Mukhtar."

"I would give my entire herd for a wife like you. Imri is a lucky man. And your heartache, mother of Uzik, is from Allah. When will your husband return?"

"I don't know," Anna replied in Hebrew.

"It is not good for a couple to be apart during the first year of their marriage. Many dangers lie in wait. Many evil powers wish to separate you."

And then Mohammed told the rest of the tale about the mukhtar's horse, which knew how to speak, and listened secretly to people's conversations. That was how the clever horse discovered that none of the mukhtar's friends were loyal to him, expect for one.

"How could the mukhtar tell which one was loyal?" I asked.

Mohammed pinched my cheek in exactly the same spot Herzl Fleischer had punched me. It didn't hurt much anymore.

"Listen well, Aza'ar. Will he who is loyal today be loyal tomorrow?"

Now I was afraid Mohammed knew everything. The "fictitious" marriage, brides for the sake of the homeland, and the second wife staying in the Bristol Garden in Jerusalem, who refused to give Imri a divorce—all the tricks and lies, a little bit of honey and a lot of poison.

I shivered. Anna turned the horse in the direction of the olive grove. The silver-gray leaves brushed against us. Mohammed gave us some fresh pita breads and the bouquet of fragrant herbs from Fahtma's garden, and leaned over to whisper some of his soft words into the horse's ear. When he straightened up, he asked whether Anna knew what her name meant in Hebrew.

After she had secured her feet in the stirrups, she sat up straight in the saddle. Shadows began to fall. We couldn't stay any longer. It would be dark soon. I held the jar of bees close to my chest. The queen bees were still. That's my Mohammed, I said to myself. He keeps what he knows to himself.

He didn't wait for her to reply.

"Anna means 'where'." Mohammed slapped the horse's flank and sent him home.

The road wound around the English base. We rode along an unfamiliar part of the fence. It wasn't the place Johnny Weissmuller liked to wander around in. The Hawkers were so close, we could have touched their wings with our fingers. The trees around us were rustling. Cypress trees and old oaks and carobs that had seen a lot of darkness in their long lives. We didn't even have a kerosene lamp. If Anna was scared, she didn't show any sign of it.

She stopped suddenly. The end of the road.

"This is the most beautiful place," she said, full of wonder.

It was dark, and Anna couldn't see that we had entered the village cemetery.

At night, it looked like a garden. There was no other way home.

The old horse made its way among the gravestones, and I said, "That's because you don't know anyone here."

I didn't go near the place where my mother and father were buried.

It was only in the movie that the elephant cemetery looked like a mysterious place. I told Anna what happened towards the end, how Jane's father, the Colonel, died after spending the whole movie searching for the wondrous place that held a treasure trove of ivory, and how Jane consoled herself and Tarzan, saying that now, her father was resting happily with the other great hunters.

I'd held Imri's hand so tight during that scene that I hurt him. I didn't know whether dead people were happy. It was only a movie.

Anna spurred the horse on. She wasn't afraid of cemeteries. She tried to take hold of my hand while I was talking.

I pushed her away. I'm not afraid of the dark, Anna. If Jane's father hadn't gone off on that long journey to look for elephant cemeteries, maybe he would have stayed alive. But then there wouldn't have been a movie.

Anna's hand brushed my head lightly. She touched Imri in a different way. I thought what she was saying was that a graveyard symbolized a chain of people connected to each other by love and hate, by anger and reconciliation, but there were words in Yiddish I didn't understand. Anna said she knew three "Annas" who had lived before her and were resting in the earth in Lutsk. Someday, she would tell me her own tales about a talking horse.

In the meantime, the photographer's horse moved slowly forward. We both understood what his neighing meant. He was as exhausted as we were. Maybe horses also had nightmares about ghosts, and didn't think a cemetery was such a beautiful place. Anna had actually managed to get hold of my hand and didn't let go. "Uzik, dead people can't hurt you more than the living." And she said something else she'd wanted to tell me for a long time, but forgot. "Johnny Weissmuller is Jewish."

Fahtma

I'll cross the river with Imad, my cousin. There, on the other side, no one will ever find us. I am not blackening the family honor, Anna, because the honor of lovers is also precious in the eyes of Allah, and what happened to us is from Allah. Fate is a mute horse, the good Idris, who cannot tell us where he is leading us. I will not give myself to a man only because of his wealth and his herds and his estate in the Galilee. I love Imad in the same way your soul is planted in your Imri's soul. I draw strength from you, as if you were a well of clear water. Even though your husband married another woman, you do not lose hope.

Of all the miraculous plants Allah created, I picked for you the bitter and thorny *doret el-acuv*, the "turtle herb," which will heal your sorrow. Listen, Anna, once there was a lonely *fellah* whose beloved had left him for his cousin. He spent that winter in his village, pining away for his love. And when spring came and he was walking along the road that led from the well to the olive tree, a turtle crossed his path in pursuit of his mate, who did not want him. And the *fellah* saw that when the turtle picked some herbs and threw them onto the back of the female turtle, a miracle happened. His mate returned to him as if she had never been away. The turtle climbed onto her back and they mated on the greening earth. Do you understand, Anna? The *fellah* knelt down and thanked Allah for his great benevolence, and then he too picked some of the turtle's herb, and hurried to his beloved. He put the herb on her back, and she never left him again. On the day Imri returns from his travels, put some of the turtle herb on his back, and he will never leave you again.

Chapter 27

There was one question that bothered me. Were Tarzan and Johnny Weissmuller the same person?

Sure, they weren't the same person before the movie, but I was trying to understand what happened *after* the movie.

I had to get things straight in my head. If Tarzan was the English Lord Greystock at first, did that mean that when Johnny Weissmuller was off the screen, he was Jewish? Anna said it wouldn't do him any good. Although his roar was heard everywhere, and the world champion swimmer was an admired figure, in the Fuehrer's eyes, he was still just an inferior Jew.

When we got home, Aunt Miriam was all over me. I thought that now, she'd call me a few nasty names and yell at me, but she threw her arms around me and held me so tight, she almost choked me. She'd been so worried when it started to get dark and we hadn't come home that she forgot to be angry.

"It's getting more and more dangerous in this country," Aunt Miriam wailed. "This is not Poland."

Anna said that the calm in Poland was like the smooth white screen before the pictures appear on it. Again, she predicted disaster. Whenever she was waiting for letters, she imagined terrible things. In the village, they called her "a prophetess of doom" behind her back.

The buzzing of a Hawker coming in to land at the English base upset the horse, and he stamped his hooves. It was completely dark now. We tied him to the side of the hen house. The photographer promised he would come and take him the next day. The horse was covered in sweat after its night ride, and I ran my hands over his stringy mane, searching for a soft word to whisper in his ear. None of Mohammed's words were right, and I stopped trying, because I was so tired.

"Tomorrow, I'll go to look for my relatives myself," Anna announced to Aunt Miriam, and asked her to let me go with her. It was the Passover vacation.

Early the next morning, we put three new queens into the hives. I explained to Anna that from now on, the female workers would devote themselves to taking care of the queen, because the future of the whole hive depended on the queen's mood. The queens had large families now, Anna said, and I saw in her face how much she missed her own.

We waited near Aharonchik's bakery for the first bus to Tel Aviv. Aunt Miriam hugged me again. I squirmed in her arms, trying to get away.

"Take care of the boy, Anna. He's all I have left in the world."

Something froze inside me. I never thought Aunt Miriam felt she had so little left. Only now did I understand that she had lost her younger sister and her brother-in-law, and except for me and Imri, there was no one else in the world she could call "hers."

Anna was wearing the dark dress she'd worn on the day she arrived, and her hat looked strange, the way it did then, when she stepped out of Zusia's wagon, so out of place.

"You're wearing bourgeois finery again," Aharonchik sighed, and Anna and I smiled at each other, knowing that we were about to hear the inevitable speech about the proletarian worker's overalls that all the Jews would someday wear as a symbol of solidarity and equality. Anna didn't look so tall, or maybe I'd gotten taller in the meantime. The last letter she got from Lutsk, with her relative's address in Tel Aviv in it, was in her handbag.

Zionka's mother was going to Tel Aviv too. She couldn't hide how happy she was when she asked Anna, "So you're leaving?" And she whispered to Mali Perlmutter, the watchmaker's wife, who was sitting in the last row of the bus, that Tonka Greenbaum had made Imri's head spin. Zionka's mother was relishing the gossip so much that she forgot about her feud with Mali. Rumor had it that Imri was not abroad on any mission, Zionka's mother whispered more loudly, but was staying in the Bristol Garden in Jerusalem with his legal wife. Someone had seen them strolling along Jaffa Street on their way to dance in a café.

Anna and I ignored them. Sometimes, I felt sorry for Zionka for having such a mother. If the English told us to get rid of an old resident in exchange for every new immigrant, I would return Zionka's mother to Warsaw, to her uncle, Max Rosenberg, who owned a velvet and lace factory, even though, on second thought, I felt bad for Zionka, who would have to talk to the air, like Aunt Miriam.

The bus was bouncing along through the citrus groves, and we breathed in the sweet smell of the fruit. Perfume, as Zionka's mother had said when she asked Imri to bring some for her from Europe. The fields were covered with yellow buttercups and red chrysanthemums, and I, who didn't have a collection of dried "flowers of our homeland," and wasn't a nature lover like Zionka, found myself half-boasting to Anna, "You see, we have spring too. It's just very short, not like in Poland."

I really hoped Anna wouldn't be disappointed by Tel Aviv. To me, it was a huge city, because any place that had a movie theater was just like a city in Europe, even if it didn't have trams or a telephone in every house. Only Zionka's mother looked down on Tel Aviv, calling it "provincial," and saying that until the day the famous maestro Toscanini came to conduct the Philharmonic, we shouldn't waste the word "city" on it.

The closer we got, the more sand there was, and everybody closed their windows because of the dust. I was a little embarrassed, because that wasn't how the entrance to a big city should look, and I assured Anna they would build lots of buildings here, but I wasn't as sure about that as our leaders were. If all the Jews in the world were like Anna's family, there wouldn't be anybody to live in them.

When the bus stopped on Allenby Street, I started to cheer up. It wasn't every place had a street named after a general, even though he was English. We had to look to the right and to the left before we crossed the street because of the cars and wagons, and the noise was deafening.

I loved walking along a crowded street, surrounded by people I didn't know anything about and who didn't know anything about me. There, I wasn't Uzik the troublemaker, but just a kid like any other. And Anna didn't look different and foreign, because Tel Aviv was like a long clothes line on which all the clothes in the world were hanging. Khaki pants and white undershirts, embroidered Arab dresses, kaffiyehs and galabiyahs, European suits and colorful ties, wide-brimmed hats and spiffy English uniforms with shiny brass buttons and belt buckles. The only thing missing there were fur coats.

—

We looked for her relatives' address. With the help of passersby, we finally reached a house near a plaza that was soon going to be built. I was sorry we hadn't taken Johnny Weissmuller. How he would have enjoyed running after cats in a perfect circle.

Anna was impatient. "Let's go," she said. Too bad, Anna, that you can't enjoy my big city.

We walked up to the second floor and knocked on the door. Anna held the letter from her parents against her chest. She looked at it every once in a while, as if she were afraid she'd forget the address. I knew it by heart.

The woman who opened the door was young, and she was holding a baby in her arms that was flinging its arms this way and that, trying to get down and walk by itself.

Anna smiled at the baby, but then her mouth fell in disappointment, because she had expected her relatives to be older.

Since she still hadn't mastered Hebrew, I spoke for her.

The young woman said, "That's right. They did live here," and invited us to come in.

Anna insisted on standing in the hallway. We heard a voice calling from inside the apartment, "Who's that?" and Anna was encouraged by the fact that the voice sounded old.

Anna held the letter out to the young woman, who pushed it away, reminding me of myself when someone forces me to read.

"I don't read Yiddish," she said, and shouted, "Grandpa, come here!"

The old man dragged his feet to the doorway. In the meantime, other doors in the building were opening, and neighbors were looking out. The baby was gurgling happily at the new faces, trying to touch me with its hands.

Anna gave the letter to the old man, and he read out loud. "Go to our relatives, Anna. They will be your family in the desert of Palestine until you decide to come back to us."

The old man said the tenants had left a year ago.

"Where do they live now?"

The old man shrugged. Palestine was a place where somebody was always looking for somebody or something.

The neighbor across the way opened her door.

"They went to America, and didn't leave an address."

Anna folded the letter, shoved it way down into her handbag and turned to go.

"Wait a minute," the baby's mother said, "they forgot something here."

We stood in the hallway, and the happy baby's gurgling echoed from the walls.

"They couldn't adjust here," the neighbor said, " and they finally gave up and left."

The young woman returned holding a torn, faded photograph.

"Are these your relatives?"

Anna didn't recognize them. Two strange people looked out at us from the photo. A happy couple.

The baby's mother said, "We found the photo in a drawer when we moved in."

Anna wanted to give the torn picture back to the woman, but she wouldn't take it.

"Keep it. That way, you'll at least have a memento."

I turned the picture over. The back was empty. Nothing was written on it.

The couple didn't look anything like Anna. Just a man and a woman smiling a broad, fake smile for the photographer, because that's what they were supposed to do, and I noticed that behind them was a table with a pair of candlesticks on it that were very similar to the ones in Anna's trunk.

The baby tried to grab the picture from my hand. It was the friendliest baby I'd ever seen.

We said thank you, and left.

Chapter 28

Anna cried. Two wet streaks lined her cheeks, glistening in the bright sunshine of the new plaza that was under construction. She covered her face with her hands. I thought I heard a voice break inside her, "I have no one here," she said.

"You have me," I whispered almost to myself, thinking, why didn't they send *me* to marry her "fictitiously." I wouldn't have divorced Anna for any homeland. I would've kicked up a storm at the Jewish Agency and broken my promise to marry four brides. The Jewish Agency people would've been furious, but I was sure the homeland would've forgiven me.

I had taken the old picture from the young woman and buried it deep inside Anna's handbag. You could say I'd had some experience in doing that. The Radoms in the sleeves of the Polish fur coat and two in Zionka's duck pen.

Anna said, "The Nazis will take over Europe. They'll be everywhere. In Lutsk too."

I remembered how my teacher had reassured us in the lesson on the Jews in the Venice ghetto, a word I'd never forget now. "Lutsk is such an out-of-the-way place," I tried to comfort her, "Who'd ever go that far?

Mohammed says that we shouldn't think bad thoughts about the future, or else we force it to wear the face of our fears."

The young woman had come out for a walk with her baby in its carriage. They were approaching the new plaza that was being built, and the workers warned her not to come any closer. I knew Anna was thinking about her little sister now. Maybe, like this young woman, she too used to wheel her sister in her carriage along the main street of Lutsk, on the banks of the river that flowed through it.

Anna said, "I'm afraid I'll never see them again."

I pulled her along with me. This wasn't the tall, strong Anna I knew, the Anna who helped an English pilot remove a bullet from Johnny Weissmuller's quivering body, the Anna who wasn't afraid of the blood. Now, I was hoping she wouldn't forget Imri and the honey. I wasn't sure that Anna was sad only because she didn't find her relatives, and I was afraid she'd start talking to them in the air. Don't forget, Anna, they're only in America, not dead.

She said that maybe she'd go there to look for them.

"And how will you start from the beginning all over again?" I asked, "how many times can you change homelands?"

Then Anna told me the tale she'd promised to tell me. "The tale of a Polish landowner whose horse could talk, but he didn't understand a word it said. Only the Jewish tenant who paid rent to live on the landowner's property because he was not allowed to buy land, listened to the horse's words and was silent. One day, the horse heard

197

its Polish master plotting to kill the Jew and steal his money. The horse went to the Jew, warned him, and said he would carry him off to a safe land where no evil would befall him. But the Jew refused. 'Horses can't talk. It must be my ears playing tricks on me,' the Jew said to himself, and did not leave the place in time."

We walked silently along the streets of Tel Aviv. Anna was carrying on a silent conversation in her mind, arguing with her family, urging them again to hurry to Palestine. I saw how miserable she was, and I pulled her along with me. There was only one consolation possible.

Even though I'd only been there once, I found the Beit Ha'Am cinema easily. I recognized the building right away. That day in the summer, I'd waited there, near the box office, for Imri to buy tickets. He was at the end of the line then, and I was afraid the tickets would be sold out. And standing there, at the main entrance, had been an usher with white hair and a welcoming expression, who had led us inside, into the darkness.

I ran across the street, pulling Anna along after me. I really hoped that *Tarzan, King of the Apes* was still playing. After all, lots of people hadn't seen it and didn't know about it.

I was ready to see the movie over and over again. I was sure that if she sat in the dark next to me and watched Johnny Weissmuller, she'd understand what Mohammed meant when he talked about the future.

We stood in front of the showcase. I checked out the pictures, which mingled with our reflection. Anna looked tall in the glass, and I stood on tiptoe. There were pictures of movies they would be showing soon. I was disappointed not to find any new Johnny Weissmuller movies. I ignored the names of the movies and the movie stars, looking only at the faces to be sure I wasn't making a mistake, and maybe in his new movie, Johnny Weissmuller had covered his naked body and had exchanged his loincloth for regular clothes.

Scenes of the movie they were showing now raced past in the showcase like the train to Haifa, on which I'd ridden only once, when I went with Aunt Miriam to pick up a package at the port. There was a couple in one picture. I stamped my feet in excitement, because the man's chest was naked, and I was sure I'd found Tarzan. But in the next picture, the actor was taking off his pants, and his thin, carefully trimmed mustache reminded me of Major Parker's. He was sitting on his bed and getting undressed next to a nervous-looking girl wearing a striped dress and a small hat. Her back was to him, but she was sneaking a look at him. The man already had his shoes off. He would soon be completely naked. They were together in a double room. It was pouring cats and dogs outside their window, and the man had stretched a rope between the two beds. Maybe they were planning to talk on a telephone made of tin cans. Examining their faces again, I saw that they looked as if they were about to suck honey, but another image reflected in the showcase window spoiled their plan.

Someone said, "It's always the same movie, little Zionist. It never changes."

Reflected in the glass were a pilot's hat and uniform, and a shiny belt buckle and glittering brass buttons. Anna turned around. "Hello, Charlie," she said.

Major Charles Timothy Parker was on leave. He thought Tel Aviv was the closest thing to London in all of Palestine. When he said that, I liked him. He offered to buy us all tickets for the movie that was playing in the Beit ha'Am Cinema. I said no immediately. I wouldn't be disloyal to Johnny Weissmuller, and certainly not with an Englishman. I had the feeling that Johnny looked out of the movie to see who was in the audience.

The same usher with the white hair and beckoning expression was standing at the main entrance, and he said to us, "The theater is full, so if you want to come inside, you better hurry up, because the movie is about to start, and you already missed the newsreel."

Major Parker said, "You should see it, Annie, it's a romantic movie. With Clark Gable."

Romantic. That was a word that Zionka's mother and Mali Perlmutter used. Once, before they argued. Zionka and I caught them dancing the tango and foxtrot together in the empty committee house hall, taking turns being the man.

Again, the pictures got stuck. Maybe I should change my mind and see a romantic movie after all. Major Parker looked at me and said in an enticing voice, "A charming little vixen runs away from her father for the man she loves, but in the end, she marries a different man. Clark Gable wins her." I was stuck between them. The movie was getting more threatening by the minute. Anna didn't say anything. In the showcase, there was picture of a bride running away, the train of her dress trailing along the grass.

Major Parker said, "Clark Gable dreams of taking her

to a desert island in the middle of the ocean. 'I am the owl that hoots in the night, I am the morning breeze that caresses your beautiful eyes.' Let's go inside, Annie. You won't be sorry."

That was the first time I was afraid of a movie. After all, Clark Gable was Anna's Johnny Weissmuller. How could you compete with such a smooth guy with a mustache? But then again, he never won an Olympic gold medal. He couldn't hold a candle to my Johnny Weissmuller. Yes, I now called him "mine," and if Johnny knew me, I'm sure he would call me "his."

Chapter 29

Anna said, "I've already seen the movie." Major Charles Timothy Parker did not give up. He tried to convince her that you could see a movie like *It Happened One Night* twice. But in the meantime, the usher had walked back into the darkness. We stood at the closed door, heard the opening sounds and, even though it wasn't Tarzan, my whole body was drawn inside.

If the Englishman was disappointed, he hid it well. How delighted he was at the opportunity to spend some time with us. For a minute, I though he'd followed us from the village, and I was surprised he didn't have friends of his own. Why didn't he spend his free time with English pilots or high-ranking officers who drank whiskey in the canteen, instead of inviting a new immigrant from Poland and a boy from Palestine to go to the movies with him?

"Do you like ice cream, little Zionist?"

I'd like to see someone give up ice cream for the sake of the homeland. Last year, at the beginning of summer, after Tarzan—thirty-one reels—ended, I asked Imri to buy me some, but he was in a hurry to be off on one of his missions for the homeland. He put me on the last bus to the village with Zionka's mother and Mali Perlmutter, who were on their way home after a concert in Tel Aviv. They quarreled the whole way.

Anna couldn't decide what to do. She looked at me. I knew it all depended on me. Although I didn't like Major Parker calling her Annie, I felt she wanted to stay a while before going back to the village, as if she wanted some consolation for not finding her relatives. And I also thought, who would see us in Tel Aviv if we went to have ice cream with the Englishman? Tel Aviv was a large city, not a small village where people were always watching and everyone gossiped about everyone else behind their back. Maybe people did things in Tel Aviv that they weren't supposed to do in the village, and maybe Anna also wanted to break the rules for once and feel the joy of playing a good prank. She even told Charlie—I still called him Major Parker—that we'd looked for her relatives, and that they'd gone to America without leaving an address.

We crossed Allenby Street, which was as busy as a beehive at the height of the season. More people walked along that street at one in the afternoon than lived in our whole village, and I wondered what it was like to live in a place where you didn't know everyone by name. Then Major Parker took us in the direction of the sea. Last year, on that day at the beginning of summer, Imri and I went all the way to the beach. We took off our shoes and socks and dipped our feet in the sea. Now, looking at Palestine's sea, I wanted to ask Major Parker where Johnny Weissmuller learned to swim. The first person to swim a hundred meters in less than sixty seconds, breaking the record. Imri told me that Johnny had been a weak and sickly boy, and when he was eight, the doctors told him to swim to strengthen his muscles.

I said to Major Parker, "Sixty-seven world records in freestyle swimming, and five gold medals in the Paris and Amsterdam Olympics. Isn't that incredible?"

Major Parker said, "You're right, little Zionist. Only very few people do the incredible."

The waves licked at our feet. Anna said she didn't know how to swim. But she'd also said she didn't know how to ride. My older brother, who was once her husband, was now on the other side of the ocean. What is he to her now?

Major Parker took us to a café. It was my first time in such a place. Everything was so beautiful. Soft music was playing, and for a minute, Anna looked happy.

An elegant waiter wearing a white jacket and holding a pad in his hand came over to us immediately, bowed, and asked, "And what will you have, sir?"

Sir. Nothing more and nothing less. Was this how Tarzan felt when he went to England for the first time?

Charlie ordered tea and cream cakes.

"And for the young gentleman?"

First "little Zionist," and now "young gentleman." When would they see me as just myself? The orchestra played soft, flowing music. Charlie stood up and asked Anna to dance a tango with him. I was sure she'd refuse politely. And I didn't know whether they danced in Lutsk.

All the ladies in the café looked at Anna. They were all wearing colorful dresses made of transparent, fluttery material, their lips glowed bright red, and they wore makeup on their eyes. And Anna, in her dark dress made of heavy material, looked out of place. She ignored them all and danced with Major Charles Timothy Parker as if they were the only couple on the dance floor. That was why I liked Anna. She was always herself, and never wanted to change because of what others told her.

The ice cream—vanilla, chocolate and strawberry—slid down my throat, cool and soft, and even though it was sweet, it didn't taste anything like honey. I looked at my distorted image reflected in the silver spoon. When I moved the spoon, their bodies moved too. I could see the way Major Parker studied Anna. He too wanted to taste her nectar, but kept himself from doing so. I was afraid that in another minute, Anna would be tempted to suck honey from him, because maybe after you taste it once, you want more, and it didn't matter from who.

She moved in a circle of dancers, a large bee in the café, her dark dress spinning around her. But still, she kept her distance from him.

In the meantime, the waiter came up to me, asked if the ice cream was good, and remarked, "What good-looking parents you have."

I thought of telling him they were two strangers who had kidnapped me at the beach because they found out I was hiding guns. I would have told him that even though I was only twelve, I knew how to shoot the newest model Radom pistol. But then I thought that a café wasn't a place for playing pranks, and the waiter hadn't done anything wrong. He was just trying to be friendly, or maybe the English pilot had really impressed him.

They came back to the table. Charlie pulled out her chair for her. He was the politest man I'd ever met. I didn't think I could ever pull out a chair for Zionka in the village committee house. And if we ever went to the movies, I wouldn't have to pull out any chairs because they're nailed down to the floor. My elbows were on the table. I knew I was breaking the rules of English etiquette, but I was raised here, not there.

Charlie didn't care that I heard every word. And maybe he wanted me to be a witness to the things he wanted to say to Anna.

"Return to England with me, Annie. We're both Europeans. You don't belong in the Levant. You and I come from the same place. People born in snow cannot live in the desert."

Charlie took her hand very gently and spread her fingers.

"Delicate hands like yours should not be stung by bees. In England, you'll be a lady. London will bow down before you. I know your marriage was fictitious. Don't ask me how. The little Zionist's brother"—and he touched my head—"is your husband only on paper."

We both turned pale. I stopped eating. The ice cream had lost its taste. The vanilla, chocolate and strawberry had all run together in a disgusting mush. I pushed the silver spoon to the edge of the table. It was filthy.

Charlie leaned over to her and promised he would never reveal the secret. Even though he was a British officer, and it was his duty to inform the government, he had chosen to be loyal only to Anna. From the moment he saw her near the fence, he knew that she was the woman he been dreaming of his whole life. I shoved the silver spoon again, and it fell to the floor with a sharp clang, but Major Parker didn't stop talking. He had to get Anna away from here. Palestine was lost. Soon, it would drown in blood.

The waiter came over, disappointed that I hadn't finished my ice cream.

"You didn't like it?" he asked, as he gathered the plates and bent to pick up the silver spoon.

We were silent. My tongue was cold.

"Your relatives were wise, and left in time," said Major Parker.

Anna whispered, "I saved my life. I fled Europe in time."

Then she looked down and began searching for something in her handbag. The English pilot had already taken out a clean, ironed handkerchief, when she came across the torn picture of the couple.

He gave her the handkerchief and practically begged, "Let me protect you, Annie."

Miriam

I fear the foreigner. His English ways are casting a spell on Anna. You must watch over her, my sister. We should not trust men who soar above us in flying machines. This foreigner might tempt her into leaving us. And the boy is attached to him too, his head full of nonsense, worthless ideas he takes from pictures, not from learned words. Soon he'll be advocating free love, without the benefit of holy matrimony. I'm still searching for a cure for him, my sister, I haven't given up.

I remember gathering him in my arms, a day-old infant, his bottle in my trembling hand. He screamed to high heaven for hours. Imri locked himself in the toolshed, his hands over his ears.

How could I have raised your children properly, sister, when I have no child of my own?

Chapter 30

Major Parker wanted to take us home in his jeep. I explained to him that it would be better for us, and probably for him too, not to be seen together. He immediately understood. Even though he was English, I liked him. And we had something in common. We both loved Johnny Weissmuller.

Back in England, the major had five dogs. A Labrador, a German shepherd, an Alsatian, a terrier and a poodle. I asked who was taking care of them now that he was stationed in Palestine, and he said, embarrassed and blushing like Zionka, that he owned a huge castle and the servants were taking care of everything. He hoped that someday, when the English and the Jews were no longer enemies, we could visit him there.

A castle? I suspected him of trying to impress Anna, but he described it with the longing of someone really talking about his home, and he sounded exactly like Anna when she talked about Lutsk.

I also asked him if the dogs missed him when he was gone.

Charlie said that Lady Mary Parker, his mother, had written to him that the dogs went out to the rose garden every morning and barked to the air.

"Someday I'll take you flying with me, little Zionist. We'll climb to three thousand feet in the Nimrod Hawker and go wherever you want, even to the jungles of Africa."

The major insisted on going to the bus stop with us. A soft evening was falling on Tel Aviv, and the street lights were lit. So what if it wasn't London. Tel Aviv was more "my" city than any other city in the world. It started to drizzle. Charlie took off his pilot's hat and put it on my head to protect me from the drops. Anna laughed. The hat was big, and covered half my face.

Major Parker said, "Do you remember, little Zionist, the first time I saw you wandering around near the fence? I thought you were a spy and Johnny Weissmuller was a code name."

Major Parker also had a story to tell. Maybe he heard it during one of his flights. An English king had a talking horse he could understand, except that they were always surrounded by mobs of servants, caretakers, toadies, and people seeking favors and charity. The horse never opened its mouth in the presence of other people, and waited for an opportunity to be alone with its master. One day, it took the king to a large, grassy knoll, and said to him, "You will lose your crown, and your kingdom will remain a small island, because you follow the people's commands and not what is in your heart." The king put his hands over his ears and whipped the horse. And on his way back to the castle, the horse threw him, and his crown fell from his head. Then he galloped off to find himself a new king and another kingdom.

We saw the bus approaching, its lights piercing the darkness.

Anna said, "Don't be angry, Charlie. If I had met you first …"

He placed a gentle finger on her lips to keep her from going on.

"I know. He's not your husband, Annie, but you love him."

Sitting in the bus, crossing the dark fields, I remembered that the photograph had been left on the table in the café. I wasn't sure it had been forgotten. I had a feeling Anna left it there on purpose.

Anna dozed, holding her handbag on her lap. There was nobody else on the bus, except for the glazier, Pasechovitch, who was bringing panels of glass for his store in the village. The windows were wet with rain and the streaks rolling down them reminded me of Anna's cheeks. I pressed my nose against the windows, which had become a kind of movie showcase. Major Charles Timothy Parker was reflected in the glass again, standing alone at the empty, wet bus stop. Large drops were falling from his pilot's hat. Then he got into his jeep, started it, and drove off.

If I put together the three stories about talking horses, I'd have a movie. A great movie. What part would Johnny Weissmuller play in it?

Anna's breathing was soft and warm. Sitting next to her, I was wide awake. The square window opposite me turned into a screen. Suppose I was watching my life, as if it were a movie. The pictures jumped around in the wrong order, because keeping to the right order wasn't necessary, and I could skip the unimportant things. I ignored the day I took my first steps and the day I said my first word. It wasn't "Mama."

The movie could start with my first prank. I'm hiding in the toolshed behind my grandfather's clay pots, and no one finds me. I hear them shouting my name at the top of their lungs, but I don't come out. Until Imri comes and gets me. He was the age I am now. He carries me in his arms, but he isn't angry.

I can shorten things here and there, or move fast forward. For example, the times in school when they couldn't teach me to read and sent me to the village doctor to check my eyes and then my head, saying that something must be wrong, they didn't know exactly what. And there was a new teacher every year who was sure he'd be the one to teach me, and the kids in the village, except for Zionka, teased me, until they finally gave up and left me in peace.

In my movie, I could change whatever I wanted. Aunt Miriam, for example, would be a happy person who didn't talk to the air. She'd dance with the rabbi, who'd be the champion tango dancer, not only of the village, but of all the Hebrew villages, and he'd also invite Zionka's mother and Mali Perlmutter to a ball in the committee house, and make peace between them. And there'd be no boring speeches made by our great leaders about the socialist vision of the future, and there'd be no Hitler and no screaming Nazis and no laws discriminating against the Jews, the "inferior race." And if I wanted to show Poland in my movie, I could use the crystal ball Imri gave me as a present and photograph a close-up of the wolf and the snow. Anyone seeing it would know immediately that it wasn't Palestine.

When I wanted it to be nighttime in my movie, I'd close the shutters and make it "fictitiously" dark, and when I wanted to show a jungle, I'd fill the picture with the castor bush that grew behind the toolshed. Anything was possible. I could even show Zionka in another ten years, tall and beautiful, her lips rich with nectar. I still hadn't decided whether there'd be any honey- sucking in my movie.

I'd move Aharonchik's bakery to the other side of the village, past the water tower, so he'd stop pestering everyone who came in for a loaf of bread with that Stalin of his. And I'd put a carved iron gate into the fence between our beehives and the British base, and add a climbing jasmine bush from Fahtma's garden so Johnny Weissmuller could go in and out whenever he wanted without risking his dog's life under the nose of the British military police.

At the beginning, I would show him as a little puppy, and then in the next picture, he'd already be a grown-up dog. That was the wonderful thing about movies. You didn't have to wait so long for something to change.

In my movie, bees wouldn't die after they sting, and the male would stay alive after it mates with the queen, and Imri would be free to marry whoever he wanted to. I wouldn't even put Tonka Greenbaum in the movie. And the *shabab* would also be cut out. I would be the one who decides.

Zionka's duck would stay a Zionist, and I'd let him peck away at as many pictures of Herzl he wanted to. After all, they printed more of them every year. And in my movie, Anna would also be just the way she was. I didn't want her to change.

Now, you can see feet. It's still not clear whose feet they are. Then the screen is filled with a closed book, and in the next picture, there are letters that turn into bees that start dancing the tail dance. Then a hand grabs the book and throws it at the Jewish National Fund box hanging on the door. You don't even have to see the boy's face to know who he is.

My mother and father could be in my movie too. And it doesn't matter that I can't remember what my mother looked like, because I could show a woman Imri's height, who's wearing a ring and has her hair pulled back in a bun. I could say that was her and everyone would believe it. And my father's heart would stop beating, but at the last minute, he'd jump up onto his feet, burst out laughing and say, "What a prank I played on you, and you believed it, you dopes."

I'd get a camera. Zionka would help me. I'd make a movie.

I only had one problem. There was no part for Johnny Weissmuller. Imri said that, walking in the street, he was just an ordinary person, like him, or me. The thought that Johnny Weissmuller might resemble me in something was ridiculous. Imri said that he and Tarzan were completely different, and in real life, he had a wife who wasn't Jane, but I refused to believe that. Nobody could take away from him those five gold medals and six world records in swimming. That's what I would tell Imri when he came back.

And the end of the movie? What would the end be?

Wait just a minute. What I was seeing now wasn't part

of the movie. The driver was shouting. Pasachovitch the glazier straightened up and his glass panels slipped down and almost broke. Anna woke up in a fright.

A fire was blazing. Smoke was billowing up from our village into the black sky, people were racing back and forth, everything was in an uproar. The bus drove quickly around the bend in the road, parallel to the British base. I saw a Hawker burst into flames, like a wounded sun that could not set. Against the background of the wailing sirens of the British military police, someone was yelling, "Fire!!!"

Aunt Miriam was waiting for us at the bus stop. "I thought I lost you," she cried, and I didn't want the end of my movie to be like this, because I hate sad endings.

Chapter 31

It was Charlie's airplane that was going up in flames. A huge, ancient castle would stand empty, and his mother, Lady Mary Parker would curse the bloody Palestine that had stolen her son.

Anna said, "Anyone who wants to return, returns. Nothing can stop him."

I didn't want to argue with her. Sometimes, when I listened to her, I thought she was really trying to convince herself. One thing that bothered me was that Charlie's dogs would keep on barking to the air.

The village was in an uproar. Fire trucks drove through our street, and the firemen connected their hoses to the water tower and flooded the main street. Aharonchik was standing in the doorway of the bakery, cursing the "damned whiskey drinkers, may their castles fall on their heads some day!"

I said to him, "Aharonchik, what will you do if you suddenly find one likeable Englishman?"

Aharonchik said he would have a serious problem. Like falling in love with a bourgeois woman, and his smile bent into a frown when he told me that after Anna and I had left for Tel Aviv, Tonka Greenbaum had arrived in the village. He'd volunteered to escort her to our house, and he even closed the bakery in her honor, something he does only on May First, Yom Kippur and the days everything closed down in protest against the British. They went to talk to Aunt Miriam, and Tonka Greenbaum demanded to see Imri. I don't know what Aunt Miriam said to her, but she somehow managed to send the second wife back to Jerusalem.

Johnny's happiness at seeing us again quickly turned into agitation. The raging fire scared him. He refused to curl up in my bed, went out into the yard and crouched there, watching the British base, and every shout of the firemen made him jump with fright. I thought he was worried about Charlie, who had saved his life. I pulled him into the house. We heard somebody shout that someone had broken into the base and tried to steal weapons from one of the arsenals. The intruder had accidentally dropped a kerosene lamp near one of the Hawkers, and the plane burst into flames. Its engine exploded and the fire spread. I remembered the guys from the van. There were things I wouldn't do for anyone's sake, even my own. I tried hard to calm Johnny down.

Smoke drifted through the cracks in the shutters. Zionka's mother told her daughter to close the window tightly, and Zionka sobbed, because she was afraid of the dark. I didn't know how a bad movie made you feel, because *Tarzan of the Apes* was the only movie I ever saw, and I thought it was wonderful, but Imri said that lots of movies flop. The audience hated them and didn't believe what they saw on the screen. During the intermission, Imri went out for a breath of air, but I didn't move from my seat. Later, I decided that a bad movie is one whose story doesn't develop the way you'd like it to. Maybe if I'd seen a movie like that, I would've left in the middle too.

Tarzan is a perfect movie. I will explain to Imri when he finally comes back from his "bride travels". What I saw in the movie was mine. If Tonka Greenbaum was looking for Imri at our house, Johnny, that means he isn't with her in the Bristol Garden guest house in Jerusalem. What a relief. I don't know what kind of husband he is now, Johnny. Maybe a husband in the air. Why does my laughter sound hollow?

Imri said that even if the beginning and the middle were bad, that still didn't mean the movie couldn't improve, and a bad beginning didn't always mean a bad end. Imri wasn't like Anna. If she saw gloom everywhere, then he saw light everywhere, and that was why I didn't know if they were right for each other. What they did have in common was that they both read a lot of books. People always pointed at me and asked Imri unbelievingly, "Is that really your brother? You had the same father and mother?"

Listen, Johnny, there's no other man in the world who would've promised in advance to marry four brides when it's definitely enough to marry two for the sake of the homeland, maybe even one. I wouldn't have agreed to any bride, unless they promised me in advance it would be Anna.

Before the curtain opened, I didn't know what to expect. Imri sat straight up in his seat. He seemed to be excited too. I felt so inexperienced when he said it was impossible to describe what a movie was. I pestered him with questions. Then I was sorry. I asked whether you could reach out and touch what you see on the screen, or whether Johnny Weissmuller was completely flat.

The seats squeaked. I squirmed in anticipation, looking around at the others who'd come into the theater. I didn't know any of them, and only after I asked over and over again what to expect, and the lights started to dim, Imri whispered, "It's like talking to the air, and somebody suddenly answers."

But he forgot something important. I was stunned when the movie started. Everything was black and white. The things I was used to seeing in color, like the sky over the village and the leaves of the castor bush, or Zionka's braids, were painted gray. At first, I was disappointed. I almost wanted to leave. I pulled Imri's hand, and said angrily, "It doesn't look the way things really are."

Imri asked if it was important for them to look the same, and he said that what we saw on the screen was a whole world that measured time differently and moved at a different pace than ours.

From that time on, I woke up in the morning and remembered that the color had gone out of my dreams, and I dreamed in black and white. I asked Zionka how she dreamed, and she said her dreams had no color at all.

—

Johnny wouldn't stop barking. I had to untie him. We went downstairs. Anna was standing at the window too, watching the flames and the smoke. She said she hated the smell and the sparks. "There's no beauty in something that burns things into ashes," Anna said.

Even though the air was giving off waves of heat, her body was trembling.

"What are they doing there now?" And I knew that Anna was thinking about her family in Poland.

I asked, "What does it feel like to miss something?" Even though I whispered it in Hebrew, Anna understood. "It's fire burning inside you. Do you sometimes miss …?"

"Who?"

Anna was silent.

I only miss Johnny Weissmuller. I don't have the courage to miss the others.

"Will you miss me, Uzik?"

I didn't promise things I couldn't know in advance. You only missed things when they were gone for good, and I didn't want to admit that anything of mine was lost forever.

Aunt Miriam joined us. Now the three of us were standing in front of the window.

Aunt Miriam said, "Tonka Greenbaum will back down in the end," and I was surprised. Aunt Miriam was talking like someone who understood what a movie was and was already planning the end.

All the residents of the village stayed awake that night. Only the chickens and the Zionist duck slept the sleep of the innocent, free of nightmares and smoke. I went to my room and shook the string that was stretched between my window and Zionka's. Her mother had threatened to separate us and report me to the British, who would deport me from Palestine. They put dangerous people on a ship and sent them to Eritrea.

That wouldn't be so bad, Johnny. I once asked Zionka

to show me Eritrea on the globe in our classroom. I put my finger on it, and saw that it was in East Africa. From there, the two of us could easily reach the jungle.

The sky was red. You couldn't see that in a movie. I whispered into the empty tin can everything that happened in *Tarzan of the Apes*, except for the scenes where Tarzan and Jane almost suck honey. Zionka was breathing on the other side of the string. She said she could see it all, and didn't need to go to Tel Aviv to see the real movie. "Me Tarzan—you Jane." Maybe that was enough. Zionka stopped me because she knew right away which scenes I was cutting, and she wanted me to put them back in immediately, or else the movie wouldn't be the same.

I can't tell you everything, Zionka. When you see it, you'll understand. You can squeeze all of time, which usually moves so slowly, into an hour and a half that goes by too quickly. I wanted to know the end right away. And you wanted to know what happened *before* the movie. Did Jane know in advance that she would meet Tarzan and that her whole life would change because of him?

You also asked if there was any danger that *after* the movie, Jane would be sorry and want to go back to the life she had before.

I didn't know about the "before," but I didn't worry about the "after," Zionka, because I knew for sure that there would be sequels. Besides, Major Charles Timothy Parker had promised me I could expect a lot more Tarzans, and I trusted him.

I also told Zionka that even in a hundred years, when Johnny Weissmuller was old and could barely open his mouth, the roar would still be there in the movie, strong and shocking, giving everybody goosebumps.

Listen, Zionka, I'm only a substitute for the real thing. Maybe everybody's life should be turned into a movie just so it can be preserved somewhere. Shortened, not really the whole story, only certain things, some more important than others, but something would remain.

Do you hear, Zionka, someone will be able to show me to my grandchildren, and say, "That was Uzik the troublemaker." And they would show Anna the way she was in 1935.

The world will look very different to the people living in the future. There'll be a telephone, without wires, in every room, and Anna will able to talk to her family every day, and maybe they'll be able to watch as many movies as they want whenever they want on a special screen that's part of the wall. That was a thought that really made me jealous. I wish I could live in the future.

We went to sleep when night had turned into a reddish, sooty morning. and Zionka's yawns were still echoing in my ear. A cloud hovered over the village, and we breathed it into our black and white dreams, oblivious to the British soldiers breaking into our yard. Johnny Weissmuller barked wildly. I thought he was wounded again. I dreamed that we were both running alongside the fence, and the sentry shouted, "Little Zionist spy!" and aimed his rifle at me.

In the dream, the blood pouring from my wound was black.

Johnny's barks were indignant. Like Tarzan, who understood the language of the jungle animals, I understood what Johnny was saying, "This is our house"—"This is our yard"—"This is our toolshed."

Then he bared his teeth, but didn't manage to bite any of the Englishmen because they tied him with a chain to the side of the doghouse.

"You won't find the weapons you're looking for," Johnny Weissmuller roared. Uzik hid the Radom. Our troublemaker is the champion prankster of Palestine.

Chapter 32

The whole village gathered around our house. The rabbi came running from the synagogue, wearing his prayer shawl. He was carrying a feather and a candle, because he'd been in the middle of removing *hametz*, the leavened bread we were forbidden to eat during Passover.

Aharonchik also appeared, the medal he'd gotten in the First World War pinned above the front pocket of his workers' overall. He was sure the English would show him respect, but they pushed him back with their rifle butts and all he could do was shake his fist at them. "You promised us a national home! You are disgracing the honorable Lord Balfour," he roared, his throat getting dry. "Your mandate in this country is only temporary. You will return it to its legal owners, you whiskey-sloshed imperialists!"

His raging Yiddish roars had no effect on them. The British soldiers didn't understand what he was saying, and continued their efficient and methodical search, overturning, breaking and destroying.

The commander said, "You Jews take the law into your own hands. It is our job to prevent bloodshed. We are not a party in your struggle with the Arabs. We will disarm all of you."

Aunt Miriam pulled at the skirt of Anna's dress. "Tell them you know... What's the name of that English pilot who saved Johnny Weissmuller's life?"

All of a sudden, the dog had a name. Until then, she'd always called him just "the dog."

Anna refused. I thought it was because she didn't want to get Charlie in trouble. The English officer in command of the soldiers repeated that they were only following orders, an expression of indifference on his pale, freckled face. The castor bush rustled. It was the only thing they didn't damage. Its leaves were battered, but hadn't been pulled off. The bush cast a shadow near the wrecked toolshed.

They came into the house, overturned the beds, used knives to cut open the mattress Imri and Anna had slept on, and scattered the straw. They even looked under the bed in my room, took out my coiled Tarzan rope and confiscated it. They didn't touch the candlestick or the fishing rod. The commander himself opened the closet door. There were all my mother's clothes on hangers, and off to one side, Anna's dresses. When they opened her dowry trunk, I started shaking. I didn't think the movie would end this way.

Johnny Weissmuller, take me with you into your movie. There, even the most frightening scenes have a happy end. Hold me tight and take me into the white screen. Together, we'll leap from one tall tree to another in the jungle.

The soldiers were flinging all of Anna's belongings every which way. They tossed out her lace pillows and her underwear. They dug deeper into the trunk, and then the clock was on the floor along with the single remaining candlestick, and even the letters she'd received were examined and confiscated by the commander.

One of the soldiers bent over, half his body inside the trunk. I knew that now, the fur coat with the newest model Radoms stuck in its sleeves would be discovered. The soldier straightened up.

"There's nothing here," he said in disappointment, and kicked the trunk, which fell onto its side.

As the soldiers were about to leave the house, the officer announced that Imri was not abroad. He'd been arrested when he got off the ship three days earlier.

Anna froze. A shriek burst from Aunt Miriam's lips and Zionka's mother hugged and supported her. I didn't know where Zionka was. I didn't see her.

Then Anna walked towards the soldiers. I thought she was going to spit at the Englishman. That's what I would've done if I had the courage. "Cowards, have you no shame?"

The freckle-faced officer towered above her. He was taller than she was. "I warn you, miss. You too can be arrested."

Johnny Weissmuller had broken his chain. He stood at Anna's side, growling menacingly, and she put a calming hand on his fur.

"Stop for a minute, sir and look at all the damage you've done. Can you live with it?"

It was hard to believe this was the same woman who had danced with an Englishman last night in the café in Tel Aviv.

The officer turned around and ordered his men to leave.

Anna did not back down.

"You can break everything here, but look around you. All of us—including you—are made of spirit. Empty air. We breathe it. It fills us, and air, sir, cannot be broken."

I was sitting in the toolshed as I had the night Imri went away for the first time. Everything was destroyed. They had even managed to dent the tin shed with their rifle butts. My grandfather's clay pots were shattered to bits. They'd torn my father's suits. One of the soldiers had really enjoyed his work. The old beehives and the tools we used to extract the honey were twisted and broken. The cover of the cache was open and the shillings I'd saved for the next Tarzan movie were covered with dirt. They hadn't touched the silver. I closed my eyes, but the picture would not change.

The Passover *seder* night, and everything here had turned into chaos.

I thought about Imri sitting in a dark cell being interrogated, maybe beaten by the English, who demanded to know what he was really doing for the homeland. I wanted to cry, but I couldn't shed a single tear.

I asked myself how Tarzan felt after Harry the Hunter shot him. That might be the only problem about the movies. When you watch one, you don't know what the heroes are feeling, so you have to guess. Did Tarzan hate the strange white creatures who spoiled the peace and quiet of his Africa? Foreign soldiers broke into my house, searched my most private possessions, and I couldn't do a thing about it, except stand there helpless and humiliated.

I forced myself to remember that there was an Englishman like Charlie, and it made me a little less furious knowing that they didn't find the guns in the end. I had no idea where they had disappeared to.

Tell me, Johnny, you went through this in one movie, and they're already filming the sequel—how do you live with a beehive that's always filling up with the wax of hate? The bees have to keep on making poison, or else they don't have a chance. I feel the poison now. It's been in my body since that day, years ago, when I was stung by a whole swarm. Mohammed explained to me that some bees go back to being wild, see enemies everywhere and sting immediately. The picture I'm trying to cut refuses to go away. A beehive surrounded by circles of dead bees, and near them, jars of honey with labels Zionka is pasting on them, "The first Hebrew *poison* after two thousand years. Made in Palestine."

Of all the pictures I'd seen in my mind, this was the one in which I was able to read.

I didn't have the strength to stand up and straighten the mess. They broke the crystal ball, too. Now I couldn't give it to Zionka. The water had spilled out, and it had a moldy smell. The snow, I discovered, wasn't soft flakes, but just little grains of some sharp, prickly stuff.

Imri was in jail, crouching in the dark, like me. What was he asking himself? Was the homeland worth everything we did for it? And the whole time, like an empty tin can, Anna's words echoed in my ears. About the orders that people, not color-blind bees, obey. Not only the Germans would follow the *Fuehrer*. The fascists in Italy, the Poles and the Austrians, the Ukrainians and the Lithuanians, the Hungarians and the Romanians, and maybe even Aharonchik's communists. Anna's Europe would go up in smoke.

I don't want those pictures. I refuse to see that movie.

What will happen to Anna's family? I don't want to think about it. The thing I'm most afraid of is myself. Of what I'm capable of doing.

Maybe someday, I don't know when, I'll try to forgive. It will take another twelve Tarzan movies for me to even decide to try, but I will never, ever forget.

Chapter 33

"Not to the air! Absolutely not to the air!" I yelled at Aunt Miriam.

I thought I'd go crazy. I couldn't let her talk that way to Imri. If she wanted to tell him something, then she should write him letters, like Anna.

I was trying to find a way to get them to the English prison.

Imad, Mohammed and Fahtma's cousin, knew a janitor who worked in the prison. Mohammed and his cousin sent him presents, jars of honey and bottles of olive oil, and herbs from Fahtma's garden, and he promised to smuggle the letters to Imri.

Aunt Miriam objected. She was afraid Mohammed would inform on us. I said to her, "I would cut off my arm for Mohammed, and he would do the same for me. If you say one more bad word about him, I'll run away from home."

When Aunt Miriam saw I might carry out my threat, she turned Charlie into a suspect. "That English pilot used Johnny Weissmuller's injury to snoop around here," she said. "He didn't bring the dog home out of humanism," Aunt Miriam said sarcastically.

"Something like communism," I commented, making her even madder.

I would ask Anna what the difference was. She'd know.

Aharonchik proposed a daring rescue operation. In the middle of the night, the proletarian masses would scale the prison walls and break inside. He stood on an orange crate, the First World War medal still pinned on his chest, and proclaimed, "We'll show the British imperialists—and the whole world—that a new race of Jews is flourishing in Eretz Israel! No more meek bourgeoisie, but valiant Samsons who will lead the revolution. Their courage will be a model for the generations to come!"

Only Johnny Weissmuller and I were listening to him. Aharonchik enumerated a list of names, "All of them Jews, Mujik, do you hear," who had taken part in the October Revolution, the one that ended the tyrannical rule of the czars in Russia. "Leon Trotsky is the commissar of the Red Army, and Zinoviev is secretary of the Third International, and Maksim Litvinov is the commissar for foreign affairs. Remember their names well. Without them, the world wouldn't be what it is. Once, in the middle of an important meeting, Zinoviev remembered that it was the anniversary, the *yahrzeit*, of his parents' death, and he apologized to the members of the Supreme Soviet, 'Forgive me, gentlemen, even though I am an atheist, I must say Kaddish.' Litvinov stopped him at the door and said, 'You don't have to go. There are ten Jews, a *minyan*, in this room, enough to say the prayer.' Why aren't you laughing, Mujik? Maybe you don't understand the joke?"

Johnny Weissmuller had left us. Now it was only me stuck with Aharonchik. He also knew which Englishmen were Jewish, and he cursed High Commissioner Samuel, who "was betraying his heritage."

I couldn't decide whether to tell him that Johnny Weissmuller could be added to his list of great Jewish people.

Aharonchik's break-in plan kept running through my mind, and I started playing around with ideas. If I could pull Johnny Weissmuller out of the movie and give him my rope and Mohammed's dagger, he would drop down into the jail from the roof, roar "Imri," and rescue him in a flash, the way he rescued Jane and her father, the Colonel. Only one thing spoiled my plan. The English soldiers had confiscated my rope.

The rabbi had a plan too. The commandment that said prisoners should be ransomed was one of the most important ones in the Torah, that's what he announced in the synagogue. A Jew could not be a slave, and it was our duty to ransom him at any price. The rabbi was even prepared to sell the Holy Ark of the synagogue, one of the most ancient arks in Palestine, in order to fulfill this commandment. He asked all the people in the village to pray to the Almighty, may His name be blessed, for the release of prisoners, and every night, there was a *minyan* to offer a special prayer for the well-being of Imri the captive.

Even though I didn't know how to read a prayer book and always had to guess what prayers were being said by reading the lips of the people praying, I was ready to join them. But I wasn't old enough to take part in a *minyan* because I still had a few months to go before my bar mitzvah.

Now Aunt Miriam was talking to the air at night too. Her conversations with my mother weren't enough for her anymore, so she was also holding long conversations with my father, giving both my parents instructions about how they could help from where they were. I also heard her talking to other dead people I didn't know. She'd gone all the way back to the first pioneers, the ones who had founded the village sixty years ago, when there were only swamps and malaria here.

I was convinced that Imri wouldn't break down during the interrogation and tell the Englishmen where he bought weapons and how he smuggled them into the country, and where the Radoms were hidden.

—

"Johnny," I said hopelessly to my dog, "don't you have even one idea?"

The days passed and, except for Imad's friend, the janitor, who was secretly passing us information about Imri, we didn't receive any sign of life.

Anna was restless. She couldn't sit by idly. She was also looking for a way. Once, she went to the Jewish Agency in Tel Aviv, and they said that now that she wasn't Imri's wife anymore, she had no right to demand visiting rights from the British.

The toolshed was rebuilt. Zionka's father came home to the village on Friday, and instead of resting, he rebuilt it.

"Where were you when all this happened?" I asked Zionka angrily. We stood facing each other, separated by the ladder her father was standing on as he worked on the tin shack. "You hid in your books, or maybe you ran off to Herzl Fleischer!"

Zionka ran home and pulled the telephone string so hard that it tore. The two tin cans fell at the same time.

She yelled, "The people who say you're a troublemaker are right. I was with the ducks, guarding the two guns." Zionka disappeared into her room and then her head of curly hair reappeared at the window. "I know why you don't read or write," Zionka shouted, "You're just afraid!"

I feel rotten, Johnny. Why can't dogs talk? Tarzan understands every word Cheetah says to him, and the elephants came to help him when he roared for them. You think my roars are a game. If my life was a movie, I could tell the audience I was sorry and say it was the wrong reel. Wait a minute, I'll just change it. Or, if worst comes to worst, I'll give them all their money back and invite them to see the movie another time.

I felt as if someone was playing a terrible prank, but wasn't enjoying it. Like when I was little, and Imri was looking for me, and I was hiding in the toolshed and laughing to myself. Now I was the one searching, and not finding what I was looking for.

I couldn't tell her I didn't mean it. I wanted to simply say "Zionka," and she'd understand. I didn't know how many reels there were in a movie, and how to tell them apart when putting them on the projector. Johnny, try to understand, I don't want to make a mistake. What I did is already done. I was standing in the yard and talking to the air.

Miriam

I have never seen a love like yours, my sister. To this very day, I don't know whether you pursued him, or he courted you. Who would have thought you'd get married. You were just children. You romped in the fields surrounding the village. His family kept bees and we raised chickens. Now, your younger son and Zionka, the neighbors' daughter, play outside, and the dog with the strange name leaps around between them. The boy talks about the future. His head is full of strange ideas. For example, that magical device people talk into that turns the sounds into a string of letters. It will save all the bother of writing. And he has another crazy idea. He wants to get a special movie camera no bigger than his hand, go everywhere with it, and turn us all into moving pictures. I ask you, is such a thing possible? After all, we wouldn't be able to prepare ourselves for this ordeal, and the people looking at our pictures in the future will laugh at us, because we were caught, God forbid, misbehaving.

I remember the two of you sitting in the yard, your legs crossed, and he, the boy who would become your husband in a few years, was describing the way bees live. You, my sister, asked why the Creator had treated them so badly, giving them so many females when only the one that was crowned queen could fulfill the commandment to multiply and be fruitful. You said you would do without the crown if you could have the man your heart desired. He, the boy who would become your husband, thought for a long while, and then said that maybe God was half-asleep when He created the bees, and so distracted that He didn't consider the results of what He was doing. He didn't think about the poor female bees who would never taste love even once in their short lives.

I am reminding you of all this, my sister, only because I'm not sure that people remember anything where you are now. Your future husband also mentioned something you learned in school. When the world is immersed in sorrow, it is forbidden to multiply and be fruitful. He told you about Noah and his sons and all the animals and birds in the ark. The Creator separated them, placing the males on one side and the females on the other, and they did not approach one another. Rest in peace, my sister. Anna says the world will soon be immersed in sorrow.

Chapter 34

When Tonka Greenbaum, that beauty from Vilnius, arrived in the village the second time, she got off the bus near the water tower and announced to the curious crowd hungry for gossip, that a distant relative on her mother's side was a leader in Palestine's Jewish community and personally acquainted with the High Commissioner's cook in Jerusalem. She assured them that Imri would be released soon. "You would do well to trust me," she said.

Zionka's mother spread the gossip. She described how Aharonchik fixed his admiring glance on the second wife, and even suggested that she come to his bakery to sit near the oven and rest up from her long, hard trip.

"Is there a telephone here?" Tonka Greenbaum asked, and Aharonchik took her to the village committee-chairman's office. Mali Perlmutter claimed she'd seen prettier girls, and Ezra Yacobi from the post office gushed with praise for her silk blouse and the gold pin on the collar.

It was too bad that whoever distributed beauty in the world wasn't a communist who believed in equality. Aharonchik's wistful sighs would still be heard in the village many years later. Even then, I thought maybe I should tell him to ask Tonka Greenbaum to marry *him*.

If I ever talked to her, I would explain that all she had to know was one sentence from the Communist Manifesto to pass the baker's test for a wife. But Tonka had only returned to the village to see Anna.

They stood face to face. Two brides with the same groom, and the groom himself wasn't there to choose.

I never found out what Anna said to Tonka. What Tonka said to Anna wasn't hard to figure out, because the whole village gossiped about it for weeks. Tonka publicly announced that Imri was hers, that she never intended to divorce him. She wasn't the second bride, but the last and only one. Tonka also advised Anna to leave the village, saying she would pay for her ticket home, to Lutsk.

"I heard you miss it very much," the second wife said to the first one. "Not everyone is suited to Palestine, and Palestine is not suited to everyone."

Anna whispered something to Tonka that no one else heard. To this day, I still don't know what.

Help me, Johnny. An awful thought keeps running through my mind. Maybe I should stop with movies altogether. Sometimes I think that even the one I saw was too much. All of a sudden, movies seem to be the most terrible prank people ever invented to fool themselves with. Now, when I'm feeling so low, I don't think the telephone was such a great invention either. You get used to talking to an empty can, and you don't always know if there's anyone at the other end. I know I'll be tempted to see other movies. I'll sneak you in if you promise not to bark. You'll be there across from each other, two Johnny Weissmullers. He'll put out his hand to you from the

238

screen and take you inside.

Was there ever a time when Johnny Weissmuller felt sick of being Tarzan? He was lucky that he could always choose another part, and if he finally decides to be only Johnny Weissmuller, that's good enough for me.

I suddenly found myself near the English fence. The dog kept looking back to see whether I was behind him, then leaped forward, dug around in the bushes, passed through them, and let out a few impatient barks from the other side. Now I knew how he had sneaked into the base the day Anna arrived. Johnny stopped barking, but was still looking tensely at me, worried that the sentry might discover us. We were separated by the fence, but I didn't climb it. Instead, I crawled through the pit he'd dug, dirtying myself, tasting earth and roots.

The two Uziks were having another conversation inside me on their hidden telephone. The Troublemaker said, "Major Charles Timothy Parker won't want to help. If I were in his place, I'd take advantage of the situation and get rid of the obstacle. I'd deport Imri to a place far away from Palestine, to Eritrea, in Africa, so Anna would forget him, and then, Major Charles Timothy Parker could suck honey in his huge, ancient castle, they would be guarded by five pedigreed dogs, not some mongrel. That was one possible ending to the movie. A happy ending, you have to admit. When all is said and done, it would be very hard to convince Anna's family to leave Lutsk and join her here. England is not a desert, and it has a future, just as it has a past."

The second Uzik, weak and pathetic, who couldn't even make out one letter of the alphabet, whispered,

"I'll go and ask Charlie for help, maybe because Johnny Weissmuller trusts him. Dogs have a special sense. I haven't forgotten what Mohammed told me when he brought me Johnny. Now I'm afraid Mohammed made it up just to make me happy. I want to believe that what's in a movie is more real than what exists in reality."

There were still signs of the fire on the military base. Someone, some "British Aunt Miriam," had tried to clean them away. The dirt had been swept up, and the trees between the hangars had been freshly whitewashed. But the scorched trunks were still visible under the whiteness. Since the fire, the English had stepped up their security on the base, and now, sentries patrolled the length of the fence. We waited for the guards to change, and started to crawl on all fours across the open field so we wouldn't be seen from the hangars or the gate.

We reached the landing strip. It was deserted. There were no Hawkers there. The clear air held no trace of smoke. The pale sky was spotted with clouds that looked like patches covering holes. If anyone's there, I thought, he's very good at concealing himself.

The scent of the citrus groves, which was always stronger in the afternoon, reminded me that very soon, we'd be extracting the first honey of the season. You could tell from the smell that the flowers were full of nectar, and that next fall, Jews in Poland—maybe in Anna's Lutsk—would sit down to their Rosh HaShana holiday dinner and dip their apple slices into choice honey, made in Palestine.

I was lying down between the bushes on the edge of the landing field, staring at the sky, dozing off a little because of the sweet smell. Suddenly, Johnny Weissmuller growled. His ears pricked up. We heard the buzz of an airplane. It was circling in the sky, waving its tail and its nose as if its prey was close, and right after that, a man in uniform appeared in the middle of the landing field, signaling the Hawker where to land.

The lights of the airplane were turned on and the buzzing got louder. I've been watching bees from the time I was born. I saw how they felt their way to the heart of the flower, where the nectar is concentrated, and I could recognize their fear of the first contact with a solid surface, as if they were safe from harm only in the air. I could sense that same hesitation in the Hawker.

The signalman spoke to the pilot in sign language, and I liked that better than reading or writing. A hand waved from the window. The face was in shadow, but I was sure that Johnny Weissmuller had found the person he was looking for.

The wheels touched down. The Hawker shook, as if it had a chill, and then slid along the strip. Before it had stopped moving completely, Johnny Weissmuller and I were surrounded by a circle of military policemen.

I heard someone laughing his head off.

"That dog. Good God. Is he still alive? I was sure we hit him last time. I thought only cats have nine lives."

Johnny Weissmuller opened his mouth and bared his teeth as if he was about to attack. The military policeman pointed his rifle at him. "I'll get you now, you evil creature, and you, boy, get out of here on the double if you don't want us chasing you too."

The signalman bent and placed a block of wood under the wheels of the airplane.

Johnny Weissmuller broke away and dashed towards the Hawker. Then Charlie stood at the open door, wearing his pilot overalls and hat and holding Johnny Weissmuller in his arms, the way he had the night he was wounded.

"Don't you dare shoot! These are my friends!"

The military policemen looked suspiciously at him, and then moved slightly off to the side, watching us from a distance, pointing at Major Charles Timothy Parker, calling him nasty names behind his back, just the way the people in the village did.

Aharonchik

This is our village, Pani Greenbaum. It's not perfect, but it's a society in the making. It is wracked with growing pains and the torment of breaking old, ingrained habits.

And I have a mission here. Someday, I will bring about great changes. If you had gotten off the bus on May First, the workers' holiday, your mouth would have fallen open in shock. Multitudes of free Jews marching behind the flag, and I the main speaker, inflaming them from the platform, inspiring them to advance with me towards the new doctrine, the revolution of the twentieth century.

Welcome, Pani Greenbaum. If you choose to live among us, we will welcome you with open arms, but not as Imri's wife. You would be doing a very foolish thing to stay married to him. You already have your certificate, and it's not a contract of slavery. You are released from the bonds of Europe, and now you are a free woman.

If you were a baker like me and spent your nights at the blazing oven, you would understand that you can make anything by kneading flour and water together. First, they are separate, different materials, but once they're mixed together, you can't distinguish between them.

Take your freedom, Miss Greenbaum, because the dough has already been baked. Black, fresh bread that gives off heat. Imri and Anna have behaved as man and wife. He has "known her," in the biblical sense. Why should you take her place in bed and be haunted by her shadow every night? Such is the sanctity of sexual inter-course—ask the rabbi—and the sanctity of the flesh is not on paper.

Chapter 35

"Did something happen to Annie?"

The two Uziks inside me reacted differently. One sighed, and the other shook his head.

I didn't know how to ask for help. It wasn't easy to ask. Jane shouted and cried, Cheetah banged on Tarzan's naked back, and my Johnny whimpered. But I didn't know how.

Charlie was out of patience. He shook me and asked, "Was Annie hurt? Did she go away? Did something happen to her family. Are they all safe and sound?"

No. It was about her husband. No, he wasn't her husband at all. What should I call him. Her ex-husband, her beloved, the one who sucked honey with her and slept on the same mattress with her?

I said, "My older brother. He's your prisoner."

Charlie pointed to the Hawker. A metal bee, lifeless, unmoving, with no mind or will of its own. Even the machine gun behind the cockpit was still.

"I can take it up into the air. I can bring it down from the air, but the air itself doesn't change."

"Will you try?" I shouted, "Promise you'll try!"

"Yes, little Zionist. You're all dreamers here. Annie too. If only she would dream of me." He sounded so strange as he started to predict things.

"You'll probably be a big Zionist when you grow up. But I think that someday, you'll ask yourself all kinds of questions. For example, was all of this actually worth it?"

But Charlie promised to help anyway. He would testify for Imri and swear that he was the most honest man in all of Palestine.

I stood across from Major Parker and wanted so badly to sting a world that made you choose only one person. I didn't understand why you couldn't love two people at the same time. One Uzik—it doesn't matter which—admired his older brother, and the other Uzik liked Charlie, although Anna hadn't sucked honey with him, and maybe that was the difference between the two Uziks. Tarzan didn't have that kind of problem. The only woman he knew in the world was Jane. Suddenly, something else bothered me: what kind of world was it if two peoples couldn't share the same homeland. I felt hopeless. The machine gun behind the cockpit was a thirty-three caliber Lewis, but I wasn't going to tell Herzl Fleischer. On that day, I finally touched the wings of the Hawker. The military policemen didn't notice how Major Charles Timothy Parker took my hand and ran it across the body of the airplane. Canvas stretched tightly over metal. I drummed my fingers on it and listened to the echo coming from the inside. This was all that was left of Tarzan's roar.

The night stretched on, and I was tense. Every rustling leaf or chirping cricket made me jump. I didn't have a rope anymore, so I tiptoed down the stairs to see if Imri was back and I sniffed for the smell of a lit Players, but the mattress was empty. Aunt Miriam, full of hope, put it on the floor near the door every night. I didn't tell her or Anna anything about Charlie's promise, so they could be surprised when Imri came home.

Early in the morning, the Troublemaker inside me started to fume, and he cursed Major Parker, that English liar who broke promises. That Uzik imitated Aharonchik's way of talking and succeeded in tricking the other Uzik to come over to his side, and they both hoped the Englishmen would spend the rest of his life talking to the empty air.

———

In the morning, Aunt Miriam asked me to come back from school early, and even encouraged me to go with Zionka, who "had a good influence" on me. I slipped out and went to school alone. No one in the world had an influence on me, either good or bad. Maybe Johnny …

Right after school, Anna and I went out to extract the first honey of the season, and Aunt Miriam went to Tel Aviv again, hoping she would find some important person in the Jewish Agency who could pull some strings with the British generals.

Anna and I put on our beekeeper suits. I loved hiding behind that costume. No one could recognize me. Anemones and poppies covered the field next to the beehives, and Anna was surprised.

"Bees are not attracted to the color red, " I told her.

She picked a flower and pulled out its petals, leaving the stamen exposed, swaying in the breeze. "Happy are the bees that don't see blood."

Sometimes, I didn't like what she said.

All kinds of insects surrounded the hives. Busy little lives. Beetles crawling in the grass, processions of ants searching for food, worms munching leaves. This is our short spring, Anna. It ends almost before it begins, and soon everything dries up.

I remember how I once ran after a flying bug. I wanted so much to train one, so I could have a pet of my own. That was before Mohammed brought me Johnny Weissmuller. Imri, who could identify every kind of insect, got scared when he saw me running after it. It was a locust. I was little and didn't understand why the whole village had come to an emergency meeting at the committee house. The children stood at the window and listened to the frightened farmers arguing and shouting at each other until the rabbi stood up and said that the Talmudic sages believed the locust was a *shoah*, a holocaust, like war, and that was why we had to fight it to the death.

"*Shoah*," Anna repeated the word in Hebrew. I didn't know how to say it in Yiddish, or in any other language.

I opened the cover of the hive. I wished the bees would come out in one fell swoop, swarm over the fence straight to the English base, and sting the military policemen and the soldiers, the pale commander with the freckles, and especially Charlie. He would swell up and no woman in the world would want to suck honey with him.

I took out the slabs of beeswax, and extracted the golden liquid into the tins. I didn't want to taste it. There was a bitter taste in my mouth. Aharonchik was right when he said we had to encourage the workers to start a revolution in the hive. Monarchy belonged to the old

248

world. We'd behead the queen and set up a just society of workers. The hive was wide open, and only one bee flew out, hovering around Anna's hood.

She didn't draw back. "Some people believe that bees are the souls of human beings on their way to heaven," she said.

"Don't believe them. There's no such thing. It's all empty up there."

Three Hawkers landed. How pathetic they looked on the ground. I asked, "What does it feel like to suck honey with someone?"

"I don't understand."

"You and Imri ... that night. I saw."

She knelt down and took off her mask. The bee flew around her exposed head and didn't sting her.

"Uzik, you're not afraid, are you? There's nothing to be afraid of."

"But you were so sad the next morning. I don't ever want to do it."

Anna hugged me. I felt clumsy in my beekeeper suit. She said, "I would never take Imri away from you. He'll always be your brother."

You're wrong, Anna. I'm not afraid. You don't lose people because they touch each other. That's not the reason they disappear into the air.

I was hot, sweating into my suit. Her suit made it difficult for her to move. If it would only snow here.

"Where is your brown fur coat? You didn't wear it even once. It was in the trunk you brought ..."

Anna smiled and took my hand in hers. I could feel her caressing fingers even through the gloves.

"The coat is in a safe place. Don't worry."

"It's not only the coat. I have to tell you something. In the sleeves …"

"Yes. I know."

A well-guarded fur coat, Anna said. I never would have guessed that it was hanging in the Holy Ark, behind the Torah Scroll.

I laughed, but Anna didn't hear. I hadn't noticed how friendly she was with the rabbi. Their conversations weren't only about divorce and the sanctity of the Sabbath. The rabbi should add the "Radom commandment" to the *Shulchan Aruch*, the code of Jewish laws. God, may His name be blessed, pulled the trigger in heaven, and never missed a shot.

I'd forget Charlie. Maybe he meant to keep his promise, but he was just a pilot who had no real power, not an anarchist who could turn the world upside down and free prisoners.

Anna and I carried the tins. The honey spilled over onto the sides, making it hard to keep our balance. As we made our way home, Johnny Weissmuller, followed by Aunt Miriam, came running towards us. I was shocked, because she was always shooing the dog away so he wouldn't touch her. At that moment, she didn't care if Johnny dirtied the whole house with mud-covered paws. She even looked happy, although Aunt Miriam's happiness was wound-up film with flat pictures.

"Imri was released today! Thank God! He's free!"

"Where is he?" I wanted to run to him. Maybe I'd finally tell him all the things I hadn't dared to say before. Imri, you're not a brother on paper.

Aunt Miriam lowered her gaze, and her voice shook. "He left the prison and went directly to Jerusalem."

If only Tonka Greenbaum could be cut out of the movie. There was no choice but to burn the strip of celluloid as if it were a locust, so no one would ever see that flop of a movie and decide that all movies were harmful.

Anna didn't say a word. She was mute again.

Fahtma

I'm passing on another plant to you for safekeeping, Anna. It is a remedy for women who hemorrhage after giving birth. Take some of these *za'atar sadna Mussa* leaves. I climbed the tall mountain to bring Moses' summer savory for you. The prophet Mussa once stood on the mountain like me, not understanding Allah's decree that he would only see the land from afar, but would never enter it. In his sorrow, Mussa wandered, weeping, across all the mountaintops surrounding Mt. Nevo, overlooking Jericho. Allah, the all merciful, took pity on him, and planted summer savory, with its sweet scent and its blue flowers, on every mountain the prophet Mussa's bare feet had trod. The prophet became intoxicated, tasted the leaves of the plant, and his pain was healed. From that time onward, those leaves grow on the summit of every tall mountain, and only they know where he is buried.

I was a young child when Imri's mother died, and I could not help. Save these leaves for the day you give birth to his children and yours. And if the labor pains are unbearable, taste of the leaves dipped in olive oil and no evil will befall you. Then you will live to raise them yourself, and together, you will have a good life.

Chapter 36

I was watching my teacher. The blackboard was a frame, and he never stepped out of it. His lips were moving, but I didn't hear a word, as if somebody had removed the soundtrack and turned it into a silent movie. The first movie Imri ever saw was a silent one, and he still preferred them to talking movies. He said the thing he liked best was guessing what the actors were saying, or making up the words himself before they appeared on the screen between scenes.

I was lucky my first movie was *Tarzan of the Apes*. Otherwise, I wouldn't have enjoyed myself. A movie where you had to read in order to understand was not for me. Imri said that Tarzan was once a silent movie, but I didn't believe you couldn't hear his roar.

Zionka was sitting in front of me, filling her notebook with cramped little letters. I wasn't writing, and I was also the only one in class who didn't pass notes during lessons, and didn't laugh at the jokes they wrote about the teacher.

This is the same school Imri had gone to, and he had the same teacher in the same classroom. Nothing had changed. But Imri, once he was free, ran straight into the arms of Tonka Greenbaum, and forgot Anna and us.

Now we were all air.

The pupils were writing, and my two Uziks were talking away at the same time inside me. If I started speaking to Zionka again, I would tell her this: "I don't know what's worse, love or movies. They both end in disappointment. In both, you get carried away like a fool, and you're both the happiest and the most miserable person in the world."

The beginning looks promising. You feel like Mohammed's mukhtar riding on his talking horse, the two of you riding towards a mysterious place, but for some reason, you can't direct the end to be like the beginning. If I were aiming the way I aim at the Jewish National Fund blue box, I would find the problem and understand exactly what had gone wrong.

The teacher called Herzl Fleischer to the board, and he wrote something in giant letters. I didn't want to be tested anymore, not even orally. At the end of the year, they would expel me and that would be that.

But on second thought, it seemed to me that love was worse than the movies.

Zionka, it would be worth your while to go to movies, but don't ever fall in love. I'm warning you only because I haven't forgotten that you are the one who guarded the guns for me.

If the Polish word for "love" is so complicated, that means the Poles must be very smart. They don't use it very much, so they save themselves unnecessary heartache. In Hebrew, it's a simple word, only four letters, and you told me it was easy to write and easy to read. But I think words like love, or homeland seem swollen, as if they'd been stung. I must explain to you, Zionka, that no one does anything for the sake of something or someone. People do things only for themselves.

Recess. Everyone went out into the yard. The boys were playing soccer, and I was stuck at the window. Even though I could see it all, I was far away from it, in a completely different place. Herzl Fleischer was storming the goal. A tremendous kick. I was sure he'd scored a goal, but because of the silence that followed, I understood he hadn't.

How to continue? The picture was slowly dissolving. The screen was empty. Just a wrinkled old rag someone tried hard to stretch tight, but ended up by tearing the edges. I put out my hand. To touch—that was the most important thing. To try and touch something. A leaf, a hair of Cheetah's tail, a thread of Johnny Weissmuller's loincloth.

There was nothing there. Even I wasn't here. I wish someone would save me from myself.

Something bounced against my back. I wasn't sure I felt pain. I turned around.

Zionka was in the doorway, throwing a paper plane at me.

It was all done in slow motion. First, her hand arcing upward, then the folded plane fluttering in the air, losing its equilibrium, crashing.

"What do you want?"

Zionka said, "The fact that I'm talking to you doesn't mean I'm not angry any more. I'm just going out for the recess."

I didn't like recesses and intermissions. I was too

impatient to see the continuation. Imri said there were intermissions so we could remember who and where we were. And of course, so the person selling candy could make a living.

"You have to hurry," Zionka said, "Fahtma was here. Mohammed wants you to go to his village right away. He has to give you something."

"I'll go after school." In the meantime, I crushed Zionka's paper plane into a ball, but I didn't feel like throwing it at her.

Zionka stamped her feet. Her braids bounced, but because of the slow motion, they looked like dancing snakes.

"Mohammed said it was urgent. You should go immediately! He said now!"

The girl next door. I didn't know whether she was a girlfriend on paper. I walked slowly, imitating the way she moved. No one was going to tell me how fast to go forward or backward. I sometimes thought that they were exactly the same.

The eye of the camera would zoom in and magnify everything. The dusty hilltops, the terraced hillsides covered with vineyards, the Sheik's tomb, the olive trees at the entrance to the village, every leaf a drop of glistening silver. "Those trees," Mohammed had said, "are a reminder of what the world has long forgotten." Hundreds of years ago, some passerby threw an olive pit on the ground, and this olive grove and later, the village, grew from it. The water well and the mosque and the vine arbor near Mohammed's house and Fahtma's herbs. I wouldn't leave anything out.

As I walked out the door, Zionka called, "I'll tell the teacher you didn't feel well. I'll cover for you."

The kids in the yard were shouting excitedly. Herzl Fleischer had scored a goal. They were cheering him. I was right on the threshold, marking it with my feet, swaying between what was happening there and what was happening here. Johnny Weissmuller was the only one who didn't hesitate to break through fences.

I unfolded the paper plane, and saw that it was made from a page Zionka had torn out of her notebook. Cramped little ant letters disappeared over the edges of the paper.

Chapter 37

The *shabab* was lying in wait for me at the entrance to the village. I recognized them right away, even though they hadn't had time to cover their faces with kaffiyehs. All of a sudden, I wasn't scared. They were just boys, just a little older than I was, and I wanted to shout "troublemakers" at them.

They let me pass along the road, only their blazing looks stinging my back. One of them skipped in front of me, drawing his finger across his throat.

"Here's Mohammed's Jew friend." Jew, Jew, Jew. A distant echo rolled around in my mind. *Żydzi!* Jews, get out! I wanted to proclaim that Johnny Weissmuller was also Jewish. It wasn't his fault. He didn't choose to be Jewish. If it were a matter of choice, maybe there wouldn't even be one Jew left in the world.

I almost stopped to tell him I'm Uzik and you're whoever you are. We both talk to the same air, drink from the same well, and hide from the burning sun, and those olive trees don't look like the fir or the birch or the oak trees that grow in Anna's Europe, and we have what we have, and we don't have what we don't have, and that's all there is to it. Nothing you could turn into a great movie.

I'm sorry to this very day that I didn't say it. Maybe it would have changed something.

Fahtma Daudi showed me the way, as we slipped quietly among the trees with their rustling silver leaves. She didn't answer my questions or assure me that nothing bad had happened to Mohammed. The innocent girl of Mohammed's tale. I always knew when she entered a room, because of the scent of herbs that emanated from her. I didn't want her father to marry her to the old man from the Galilee just because he had a hundred goats to give for her hand, and I hoped she would be lucky, like Jane, and get to choose her own Tarzan.

It was cool in the grove. As we walked, I filled my pockets with unripe olives. Mohammed was waiting near the last tree, the one that grew closest to the wadi. That was the one people meant when they said that hundreds of years ago, a passerby threw a pit onto the ground, and the whole grove, and later the village, grew from it. A donkey piled with twigs was tied to the tree. The sting inside me started working.

"I have to leave here," Mohammed said. "There is going to be a war, and neither side will back down." He had found the guns in the beehives a long time ago, but hadn't turned us in. Loyalty is not a word only for horses.

"Don't hate, Aza'ar. Hate is a poison more terrible that that of the bees. It destroys you slowly. Someday, I don't know when, people here will understand that they have no choice but to grit their teeth, back down, and live together." And then he repeated that first, blood would be spilled.

I wished I were a colorblind bee. I remembered what

Anna had said about blood and its price.

Mohammed took a jar of new queens from the donkey's back. There, across the river, he would harvest his own honey, and the Jordan would be the fence that Johnny Weissmuller wouldn't be able to cross. The gang had threatened Mohammed. They'd caught him smuggling Imri's letter from the prison. He didn't join Az a-Din el-Kasam, the fanatic from the Gilboa mountains who was always inciting the people to massacre. "You and Imri are my brothers. My hand will never touch a dagger."

There was a huge lump in my throat. I hadn't said goodbye to my father. Even when his body was twitching, I couldn't say goodbye to him.

I was choking. "Mohammed, I'll never see you again."

"Maybe your children and mine, Aza'ar, or our grandchildren, or great-grandchildren, will meet one day …" I made him stop talking. His words were too sweet. I didn't have the kind of imagination he did, and it was hard for me to see myself as a father.

We are beekeepers, Mohammed said, the healthiest people in the world. God blessed us with sharp vision and the ability to produce many children. We will bring many boys and girls into the world. Maybe we'll give jars of honey to the Arabs and the Jews in Palestine, and we'll offer the British a taste too.

"Pretty words," I said, "very pretty. The kind they always write in books."

"What do I know. I'm only a simple *fellah*." Mohammed wrapped me in his strong arms, and I hugged him and held my feelings inside, deep inside.

"Take this and give it to Anna."

It was the last letter Mohammed would smuggle out of the prison.

I whispered into his soft kaffiyeh, "He went to Jerusalem. He didn't even come to say goodbye to us."

"The letter is important," Mohammed said firmly. "Your brother wanted it to reach 'the mother of Uzik' immediately."

"I know what it says. He chose the second wife. Anna will leave, like you, and I'll talk to the air."

My head was starting to hurt even before I looked at the letters. I hurled the letter, along with the unripe olives I'd picked, at the last tree, which was also the first one. I missed. My hand was shaking. I felt Mohammed starting to get angry. He picked up the letter and wiped off the dirt and dust with his hand. "If I could read Hebrew, I could explain to you how important this letter is."

The last promise he got out of me was that I would eat a large spoonful of honey every morning. Every time I harvested honey, I would try to distinguish between the visible sweetness and the hidden bitterness. The queens were buzzing in Mohammed's jar. They wanted to be on their way. I didn't know what kind of society would finally be established, or whether there was anyone who could avoid the collision. I did eat honey, not only because I promised Mohammed, but because honey has the power to lengthen life, and I thought I'd have to live to a ripe old age if I wanted another opportunity to wrap myself in the mukhtar's kaffiyeh again.

Homeland in Arabic is *el-vatan*. I won't ever forget, Mohammed. I swear.

He didn't have time to say goodbye to Johnny Weissmuller. The dog wailed all night, and refused to come into the house. I didn't know dogs could cry. Animals didn't cry in the only movie I ever saw. I didn't know whether the horse in the story Mohammed made up especially for me could cry. Now I didn't have anyone to ask.

Johnny Weissmuller barked to the air all night, and all the nights that followed.

Mohammed

You ask difficult questions, Aza'ar. How do I know whether it's possible to foresee the future? Does the future have a picture? I've been a beekeeper all my life, and I don't know how to answer even simpler questions than those. Allah has not revealed why the bees abstain from sleep and what drives them to draw nectar so stubbornly, to devote themselves to one queen, to save the last drops of honey they have gathered for her, even if it costs them their lives. A bee needs only a few flowers to satisfy its hunger, while it tastes three hundred. What is the purpose of all the trouble, the endless work it takes to amass a storehouse of honey it will never taste.

The future is a bee, Aza'ar. Like the future, it is determined to attain its hidden desire, and no calamity will keep it from doing so. No frost or hunger in the land, not even the arrogance of man, who injures them so recklessly in the crevices of the trees. Even if the whole hive is destroyed and only a small number survives, the bees will build their home anew.

If the future is a bee, that's only because it is thinking of its offspring when it is procreating. Bees devote their entire existence to the next generation, never to themselves. Your father and mother made you during one night of love, so that even if they are in a different world, something of who they were still remains. They are inside you, Aza'ar, even if you don't feel them this minute or the next. Allah, in his wisdom, created you in such a way that you can sense only yourself.

Don't look for a picture for all the things in the world, because not all of them have a shape, a form or an image. And if you are determined to find some kind of picture, go to the well, Aza'ar, put your face close to the water and look carefully at it. There is the picture of the future.

Chapter 38

I ran, breathing like an animal, and with every step I took, I felt pain in parts of my body I never knew existed. Every stride took me further away from one place and closer to another. I didn't know whether I'd reach the place my legs had decided to take me. They insisted on moving forward, as if they had a will of their own, while my anarchist mind was moving in the opposite direction—back towards Mohammed Daudi. I imagined him crossing the Jordan, tramping though the desert sand. I could see him talking to his donkey, laden with bundles, but the donkey, which wasn't a horse, didn't answer.

The olive trees, the hills, the well and the mosque raced past me at twice the normal speed. I couldn't take in the details that were becoming increasingly blurred, getting drawn into each other, intermingling. I passed the grave of the Sheik. None of the wishes I'd made there had come true.

I wanted to drink something, but I dared not stop for even a minute. I no longer felt the pain. It was hard to know what was more real—the scene in front of me or the one behind me, which I was tempted to take an occasional peek at. These days, no one remembers the name of that Marathon runner, only the name of the place he took off from. Now I'm the runner bearing the name of an Arab village who must reach a village with a Hebrew name, and the distance is less than forty-two kilometers.

I took a short-cut through our village cemetery. Now, even the gravestones, small white squares, raced past on either side of me. Here and there, through the corner of my eye, I could see the glow of a memorial candle or a bouquet of withered flowers left over from a funeral slipping past me. I didn't linger near my mother and father's adjoining graves that we visit once a year, when Imri and I say *Kaddish* and I feel nothing. Only the blazing sun on my head. The rabbi would sing "*B'maalot kiddushim v'toharim,*" and I didn't think my father and mother were "holy and pure," like the prayer says, just because they were dead.

My true feelings never emerged when I stood at their graves.

Even though I moved closer to them, they backed further away from me and I couldn't keep them near me. Mohammed would cross the river, Anna would travel overseas, Imri would remain in Jerusalem, and only the two Uziks would stay in the same place, with Aunt Miriam to tell them apart.

I wished I were in a movie so I could cut out the unnecessary distance, but I wasn't, so I had to cover every inch of the way.

There, in distant Hollywood, they stop the camera to keep Johnny Weissmuller from getting tired, and tell him,

"Now you're here, and in the next picture you're already in the place you wanted to get to." I'll never be Johnny Weissmuller. He won four gold medals in the Paris and Amsterdam Olympics and I can barely swim across the irrigation pond.

For a minute, I almost lost the letter. That good-for-nothing wind snatched it from me. I began chasing it, but then slowed down, tempted to forget the whole thing, to let it go once and for all.

But the wind seemed to regret what it had done and rolled the envelope back towards me, dropping it almost under my feet. I stopped only to pick it up and push it securely into my pants.

I was covered with dust. My eyes burned. I didn't want to fall. I would pass on the message, even if it wasn't one of victory. One day, I would go down in the annals of the history of Palestine as the runner who pushed himself beyond the limits of human endurance only to bring news of defeat. But even so, I didn't want to fall before the finish line. The idea that Aunt Miriam would one day talk to me in the air ...

I'll make it. I *will* make it.

———

The main street of the village was business as usual. Aharonchik was ambushing customers in the doorway of his bakery. The post office was deserted and even the committee house was closed. Zusia the wagoner was parked in front of our house and I saw Anna in her dark dress lifting her trunk onto the wagon.

I could hear Aunt Miriam telling her she didn't have to

leave, whatever Imri had done. "Even if he was married to another woman, you're part of us now. Uzik and I are your family."

Zusia pushed the trunk further onto the wagon. I had to make time move more slowly at all costs. I still had to return the second candlestick I had stolen. I couldn't let Anna go without it, because then she would have no hope left at all.

Taller than Aunt Miriam, Anna bent to hug her. Aunt Miriam muttered something, and I was horrified. Anna hadn't even gone yet, and Aunt Miriam had already begun talking to her in the air.

I wanted to shout, but I was in a silent movie now. Only my legs were moving, and my arms with them, pulling the letter out of my pants. I waved, apparently looking so ridiculous that they stared at me as if I were an airplane suddenly descending from the sky.

Anna. Anna. Anna.

She had already placed one foot on the wagon. Zusia took up the reins and the horse stamped its hooves. Anna means "where" in Hebrew. Even if I managed to roar like Johnny Weissmuller, it still would've been a silent picture.

Anna's lips were moving, and I could read the words, "Write to me, Uzik. Please write."

I wanted to shout out the only two words I knew how to write. I had been practicing them secretly for years. No one knew, not even Zionka. They were the only words I had ever said to my mother in the air.

Come back!

I unfolded the letter, tearing the envelope. The light of the sunset falling upon the page colored it red. The words slowed down and then came to a standstill. Everything stayed on the page, unmoving, as if the cover of the arms cache had been lifted, and I could clearly see everything inside. I roared out to Anna the words written on it. In Hebrew. Not Yiddish or Polish, because I was sure she already understood.

"My love, my Anna. Tonka Greenbaum has agreed to give me a divorce. I am going to Jerusalem before she changes her mind. I shall come back to you a free man. Wait for me. Come back!" I didn't blush as the honeyed words dripped from my tongue. If I had known that Zionka was standing there, I would have cut them off instantly.

Major Charles Timothy Parker

When you read this letter, I shall already be beyond your borders.

A rainy England greeted me the moment the wheels touched down. You want nothing of my castle or my Hawker. I fly in the sky alone, large drops of rain falling from above, beating on the canvas. I converse with my hawk, and it replies with the wheezing of its engine. Perhaps that is the fate of pilots doomed to be alone. No woman would consent to a bird armed with a machine gun competing for her man's attention. Every time I walked out through the gate of the base, the sentry saluted me and said, "Here's the major who prefers the company of dogs to the company of women," and I smiled and said nothing. The little Zionist was right when he said that there was no substance to letters. After a while, they fade and their meaning is lost.

If I were a king, I would give up my crown for you. In England, a king cannot rule if the woman at his side is a divorcee. Even if you really were only a "bride on paper," I would lose my right to reign. I would gladly toss my crown to the wind and follow you into exile.

Be happy, Annie, for me too. And burn this letter.

Chapter 39

I was still swaying on my legs, two slivers of wood that don't look anything like olive tree trunks. I could barely stand up. I didn't hear anything, not because I was in a silent movie, but because the whole village was standing around me, cheering thunderously.

"He can read! He can read!!!"

Zionka was the first to notice and shout, and even Herzl Fleischer applauded. I was surrounded by all the people I knew from the time I was born, the ones I loved, the ones I hated, and the ones I ignored. My teacher and the principal were there too. Now they wouldn't expel me. What a shame. They'd force me to take written tests, like everybody else. And instead of being an anarchist in their eyes, I'd just be someone who obeyed the rules and did what others did, never challenging, never defying.

Later I tried to convince them that it was a one-time miracle, and when I stood at the blackboard, I pretended to be confused. But everyone nodded and said indifferently, "We know your tricks, Uzik," and they didn't even add "the troublemaker."

We were still standing at the door. Anna in her dark dress, and Zusia the wagoner complaining about the delay and warning that they had to leave before the curfew. In the uproar, we didn't realize that someone was standing among us, looking for a small crack through which he could enter. The toolshed had cast a shadow over him. Only Anna felt his presence. A tremor passed through her body, and then she froze, one hand on the handle of her trunk, the other in the air, as if she wanted to hang onto or lean against him.

The air was not empty. It was filled with Imri. Thinner than I remembered, and pale, his hair was long and unkempt, his cheeks covered with stubble. At his feet was our father's old valise.

The end. What kind of ending do I want to choose, as if I could choose one at all. The person who wrote the one word I knew how to read, right on the last picture, already knew how the next movie would begin. The word burst forth—an aggravating, annoying bug—as the lights came up in the theater, because the projectionist was impatient to rewind the movie and show it from the beginning.

But I didn't want it to be over. And despite my terrible sorrow that it would all soon end, I managed to postpone the final moment.

In the meantime, the three letters swam towards me, "E-N-D," growing larger, taking over the screen, and then imprinting themselves on the pupils of my eyes, still flickering, even when light flooded the theater and erased all traces. I blinked. I didn't want to go home.

Where is home?

Lutsk or Palestine, an Arab village or Trans-Jordan, or maybe a desolate castle in England, or the empty air.

I didn't want to choose. If I chose, I would be lost.

Anna was holding her boat ticket. Maybe that was what the famous British certificate looked like. A piece of stamped paper that decided your fate here or somewhere else, and without it, you were forced to prove that you exist. I still didn't know whether Anna had intended to go to America or back to Poland. And maybe she'd been convinced it would be better for her to go to England with Charlie.

One way or another, she stayed.

Imri dropped the valise and walked towards her. He released the horse's reins, patted its back and sent Zusia the wagoner on his way. And when the wagon moved, Anna and Imri were close to each other, separated only by a sliver of air.

Johnny Weissmuller jumped on me and knocked me over with his licking. I told him proudly, "The Marathon runner didn't collapse. A dog knocked him down with happiness."

It was only because of Johnny that I missed one scene. I didn't know whether Anna fell into Imri's arms, or whether he gathered her up to taste her lips that were so rich with nectar.

It was a scene that would never be mine, although I was sure it took place. I couldn't see it because someone blocked for a minute what was happening there in the movie, but I could always fill in the missing scene. Or maybe there was no way to fill the void, because a scene wasn't a stolen candlestick you could return and apologize for, and what I didn't know was just as important as what I did know.

Actually, what did it matter if Anna fell into Imri's

arms or the opposite, or when exactly they came together. I thought they both knew that what had happened between them could have ended in separation, although, years later, they would both discover that at that moment, Anna had separated for good from her family. And years later, I would discover Imri as a friend, not only an older brother.

I remember very well what happened next. How I said to Johnny Weissmuller, "Even though I'm the runner in this story, I stayed alive. You'll never have to bark to the air."

Maybe love, as Zionka said, was an easy word to write and to read, but I wasn't sure you could always take aim and hit it. The troublemaker inside me always insisted on raising doubts, because a word sometimes describes the opposite of what it meant. Even if they fooled themselves into believing that all the problems were solved, and the boy wouldn't be completely illiterate, I still wasn't sure that the words weren't just "fictitious." I recognized all the letters in Zionka's dictionary, and for some reason, I didn't feel that the words became truer because I could read and write them. I wrote "for the sake of the homeland" on the blackboard just so I would get a good final grade, but I still wasn't convinced. And I could also write my name and add the nasty names they'd decided to erase, the ones only I remembered.

———

I didn't leave my room that night. Zionka found my rope tossed in a corner of their yard, and I could slide down it again. The British didn't realize that it was Tarzan's rope, and just threw it away, but I didn't need it that night.

I stayed in my room with Johnny Weissmuller. I covered us both with my blanket, whispering soft words to him. Outside, a hot, early summer breeze was blowing, and there was another rustling sound. The two empty tin cans shook and clattered between my window and Zionka's. She had reconnected our telephone. I didn't pull the string and I didn't talk into it. It really was a magical device. What you say goes directly into the ears of the person you want to hear it, and you can't avoid listening.

"Now, we'll be quiet," I whispered to Johnny Weissmuller. The two of us in the dark, between what had ended and what was just beginning. And no one was allowed to disturb us.

Uzik

Since then, color has been added to movies, and today, even weddings are filmed as a matter of course. Anna and Imri's wedding was nothing out of the ordinary. It had a wedding canopy, and witnesses, and the seven blessings, and the broken glass, and even the wedding rings that had once belonged to my parents and had not been buried with them.

Imri didn't buy Anna for the price of a hundred goats. He won her hand for nothing. She was his first bride and his last, and everyone did their best to forget there had been another one in between.

"We who have been commanded concerning prohibited relationships." I remember asking the rabbi what that meant, and he turned his back and called me "a rebellious child," and there was no affection in his voice. I was filled with surprise. After all, most of the time, the rabbi had been eager to satisfy my curiosity about the laws and commandments, and it was that question about prohibited relationships that angered him. He scolded me, "That's not for you. Wait until you grow up." And the way he said "grow up" made it sound like a threat. I almost told the rabbi how I'd seen, with my own eyes, Anna and Imri sucking honey, body to body. Sometimes it's too sweet, and sometimes it turns into bitter poison.

The guys from the van stood on the side, whispering with the man from the Jewish Agency. They already understood that Imri wouldn't complete his mission to marry four brides. The homeland would have to be satisfied with two. There are some things you can do for it, and some you can't.

Imri broke the glass perfectly. A beautifully aimed and executed stamp, as if he had practiced during the long winter nights on the Jewish National Fund box. Or maybe it was only because he had practice taking part in wedding ceremonies.

There's only one picture left from their wedding. The photographer tied the scrawny old horse to the castor bush behind the toolshed and spent a long time focusing his modern camera—not a wooden box with a black curtain he had to hide behind in order to take a picture—and placing all of us in two rows.

Imri is wearing our father's old suit, and even in the picture, you can see that the sleeves are too long. His hand is creeping under Anna's white dress. Soon, they could suck honey to their heart's content. If I look at that picture for too long, it seems to be moving. Even Aunt Miriam's lips, that talk to the air, are moving.

I'm on Anna's left, squirming in the pressed, long pants Aunt Miriam forced me to wear. Too bad you can't see me, because at that instant, the Zionist duck was walking across the yard, attracted by the refreshments, and Johnny Weissmuller took advantage of the opportunity to bark loudly and send him running back to Zionka's yard.

Although there is no proof, I know I am there, outside the frame, next to Johnny's tail that was caught in the picture without me.

You can see Zionka very well. The whole time the

photographer was busy preparing, your grandmother didn't budge, her smile frozen on her face, as she waited expectantly for the longed-for moment. Behind her are her mother and her father, who came especially for the ceremony. Zionka's mother is scowling because, at the last minute, Mali Perlmutter's name was added to the guest list. Mali, who'd once been her best friend, had become her sworn enemy. Even when I'd grown up and left the village, they still hadn't made up.

Aharonchik is particularly noticeable, because he's standing on an empty orange crate, carrying a book and waving it menacingly at the sky. From the beginning, he said that it was only for the sake of Aunt Miriam, who was finally getting a bit of happiness, that he was violating his principles to attend a religious ceremony, because he believed religion would always be the "opium of the masses."

On the wedding night, the guys from the van recruited the baker into their service, and the next morning, Aharonchik left for Europe to marry a woman. He vowed to seek a loyal communist for himself and for the homeland, but finally settled for a bourgeois woman from Cracow who wasn't the least bit beautiful, with whom he spent the next thirty years of his life.

The rabbi listed in the *ketuba*, the marriage contract, all the things the bride had brought from her parents' home, and I asked him to add two copper candlesticks. I had thrust the stolen one into Anna's hand when her face was covered with a veil. It was a good opportunity to apologize without having to stand shamefaced before her admonishing eyes. And I didn't have to write the words on a piece of paper. To this day, I'm not very good with words. Throughout my life, I've managed to avoid writing and the written word, but I talk on the telephone for hours.

I still hope to live to a ripe old age, so I make sure to eat honey every morning. Perhaps somewhere, Mohammed is watching my movie and knows that it's me. His village no longer exists. The gangs were in control for many years, and the grim prophesies of my friend Mohammed Daudi were realized. Az a-din el-Kasam was shot by the British, but his name has never been forgotten. In the end, the Arab village was wiped off the map, and today, there is a kibbutz where it used to be. Even so, I know exactly where we stood that day. Near the first and last olive tree. A pit discarded by a passerby that grew into an entire grove, Mohammed had explained. Sometimes, I go there from Tel Aviv just to check whether the tree still stands on the rise of the wadi. The grave of the Sheik is still there too, although at my age, one no longer makes wishes. Do you remember, little one, that I once took you there and you made a wish instead of me? Maybe, since you're my oldest grandchild, it'll come true.

I rewind the movie, look at the pictures again and again, and Mohammed's words, "Blood will be spilled here," send chills through my body, arouse the dormant poison. Yes, I too have been contaminated.

Later, sitting in the silence, I roll the movie backwards.

There I am, a child, running towards the Arab village, not in the direction of our home. Mohammed crosses the Jordan on his way back, and instead of parting, we unite.

And even though everything appears to be moving backwards, every time I run the movie, our hug is still a hug. This angle, that one, it doesn't matter. Each time, I'm gathered up in the softness of his kaffiyeh, choked with tears. Who else in the world will ever call me "Aza'ar?"

Mohammed Daudi and his sister, Fahtma. Who can tell me whether she married the Tarzan she loved, or spent her life in endless longing? Who will reveal the rest of the story?

I'm no longer a child, and I've already had other dogs named Johnny Weissmuller.

After The King of the Apes, there were six more Tarzan movies, and around the time the seventh one reached the theaters, Major Charles Timothy Parker's plane was hit. Charlie was leading a squadron of Lancasters in a Royal Air Force bombing of Dresden, Germany. I don't know how Anna found out that, after his death, he was promoted to the rank of Colonel and awarded the medal of honor for "unusual courage, bravery and devotion in action against the enemy." She wrote a letter of condolence to Lady Mary Parker in England on the death of her son, the Colonel. In my heart, I continue to call Charlie, "Major Parker."

He once said that the branch on which a swarm of bees chooses to make its home becomes a symbol of love. Do I lack love, or do I perhaps have an excess of homeland? Sometimes one fills you up at the expense of the other. But it's all raw material, little one. Perhaps that's why I never have to write a screenplay.

How sorry I am that Charlie missed Johnny Weissmuller's five additional roars. We could've gone to the movies together. In Tel Aviv or London, or even Africa. Tarzan's roar echoed throughout the world, except in the countries Hitler invaded. The Nazis succeeded in pinning a yellow star even on the thin strip of fabric that hid Johnny Weissmuller's naked loins.

Anna continued to write letters to her family in Poland even after the war broke out, and only with the passage of time did she begin talking to the air. There were never any replies to her letters. A survivor from her hometown of Lutsk told her how all the Jews had been herded into the ghetto and burned alive. Not one member of her family survived. For many years, I regretted not having returned to that café in Tel Aviv to get the photograph we left there. Maybe the couple in that picture really were Anna's relatives. We never did locate them in America. They had been swallowed up in a crystal ball like the one Imri once brought me from Europe.

Anna would occasionally whisper to her children that she missed home, a word she never dared put on paper. There is an entire dictionary of words it would be better never to write down.

I remember how I stood outside the Beit Ha'am Cinema in Tel Aviv, hand in hand with Imri, refusing to leave. I was a child then. I didn't know how to decide on an ending for the movie. Was this a happy one? After all, even though Jane Parker's father lost his life on a journey to Africa, she and Tarzan did stay together in that primeval, virginal jungle where no human being had ever set foot.

I begged Imri to decide for me, so I could sleep in peace and have dreams as white as the screen is before the pictures are projected onto it. Imri couldn't help me. If the movie had been in color instead of black and white, we might have known the answer. I was lucky not to know then what Johnny Weissmuller's end would be. An aging actor gone mad, institutionalized. He used to roar in the corridors, frightening all the poor souls in the institution, until he was finally thrown out.

I never told you, little one, that the roar was a special effect, a combination of the cry of a hyena, or a camel, the bark of dog, a soprano's high "C," and the vibrato of a violin's "E" string.

Well, at least it had a dog's bark.

I stroke Johnny Weissmuller's silver-streaked fur. On nights when the wind whistles, I call him to my bed, frightened that when the day comes, I won't recognize Mohammed Daudi. Only you, Johnny Weissmuller, with your special dog sense, will know him.

Did we have a good life? Anna and Imri? Those who are still with us and those who are in the air. Have our lives been full or empty? I don't understand his gentle barks. Although I never learned animal language, I do know that he's trying to tell me something.

In the dark, the dog and I cover ourselves with the blanket, imagining the endings of movies. As I run my fingers through his soft fur, I feel the scar he inherited. He closes his eyes. The last Johnny Weissmuller.

www.ingramcontent.com/pod-product-compliance
Lightning Source LLC
Chambersburg PA
CBHW051531260626
47170CB00003B/886